A BAD DECISIONS NOVEL

CAGED

BY THE STRANGER

DIANNA ROMAN

WILD ONE PRESS

For information address diannaromanbooks@hotmail.com

Published by Wild One Press
Cover design by Wild One Press

Editing by Jennifer Green
Proofreading by Margaret Neal

ISBN: 978-1-959553-36-6 (Trade paperback)
ISBN: 978-1-959553-35-9 (NSFW Cover Edition)
ISBN: 978-1-959553-34-2 (ebook)

CONTENT ADVISORY

This is a work of gay erotica fiction and is not intended for readers under the age of 18. This story contains the following elements, please read at your own discretion:

- Explicit consensual sexual content
- Adult sex club
- Gloryhole
- Dubious placement of a chastity cage
- Male chastity
- Explicit adult language
- Homophobic family member
- Feelings of self-doubt
- Sexual awakening
- Elements of coercion

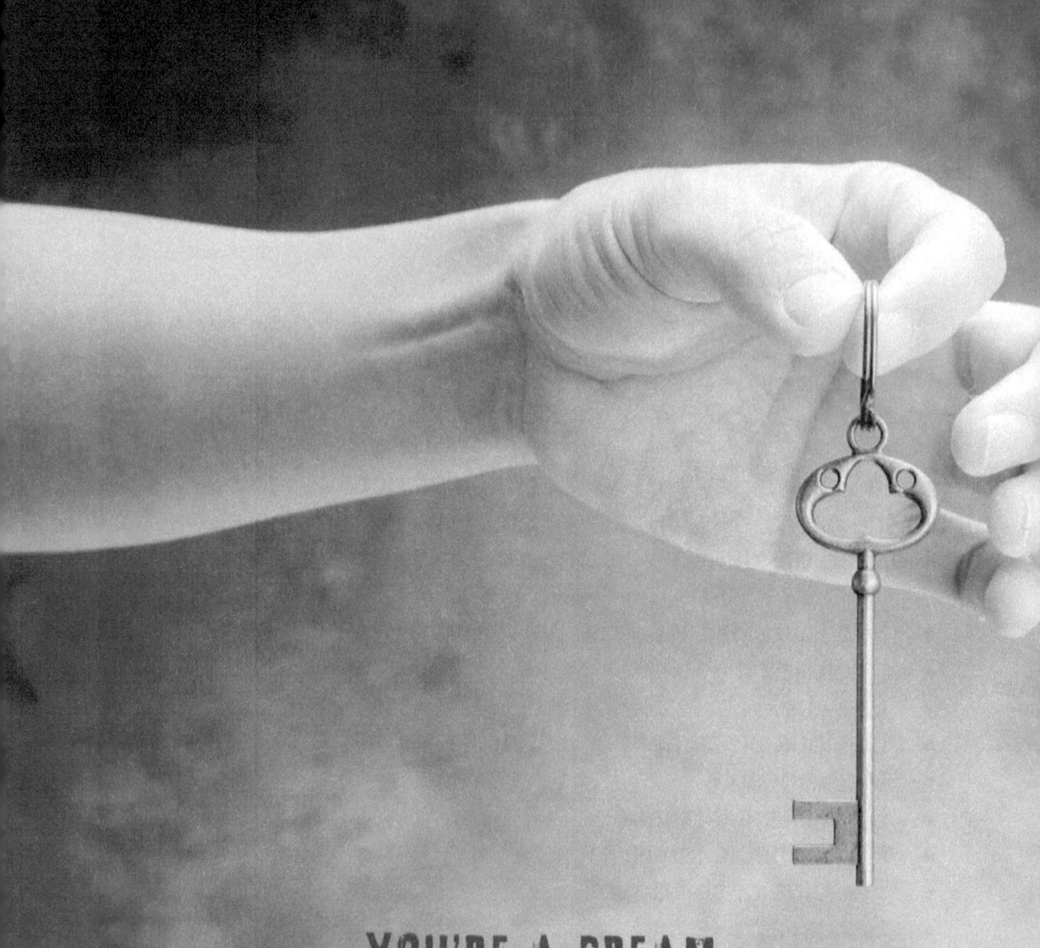

YOU'RE A DREAM
THAT NEVER ENDS, CHARLIE.
I DON'T EVER
WANT TO WAKE UP.

CAGED

BY THE STRANGER

DEDICATION

*Life's too short to not let yourself
be who you want to be*

CHAPTER 1

The doorman grants me entrance after I provide the password. The thump of the music deep inside hugs me as I step into the dimly lit vestibule.

"Haven't seen you in a while," he greets, the blue overhead light reflecting off his bald head and leather vest.

"Work," I explain absently, glancing through the open door to my right that leads to the lounge area. My pulse is kicking as usual with the ever-present worry I'll spot someone I know. I got the card for this place from a guy at a work convention, after all.

The doorman studies my ID intently and then levels me with a suspicious stare that I can't decide whether it's meant to intimidate or is genuinely scrutinizing. How frequently does someone have to come here to be deemed trustworthy? Who has that kind of time or…need?

"Lots of work," I insist, clearing my throat when he finally returns my ID.

I've never had an actual conversation with him. I shouldn't have to. He's here just to monitor admittance, not chat people up who come here for discretion.

His twinkling eyes canvass me from head to toe curiously. I don't like his unabashed eye contact or his smug smirk. I come here for no eye contact, not to be examined, although I suspect he's just being 'friendly.'

"Room three is ready." He gestures with his head to the closed door to the right. "New one tonight. It'll be just a minute, but you can go on back."

Watching his beefy hand pick up the receiver of a red land-line phone, my heart skips a beat. I know it means he's calling for whoever will meet me in room three. It's oddly fascinating that the mere push of a button can summon someone for carnal pleasures.

Swallowing back the lump of excitement in my throat, I nod and push through the door with my sweaty hand. It's only my third time here. I talked myself out of coming a dozen times after Rory, that odd sales manager from the Seattle convention, slipped me a business card to Illusion this fall.

I fucking panicked that he caught me staring at a guy in the middle of the after-dinner mixer, brushing off his implication. The balls on that guy. I didn't think I was that obvious.

In the grand scheme of things, I don't give a shit what anyone from the company would think about my sexual preferences. I have neither the time nor the desire to pursue anything. I'm not a relationship guy. Something about getting to know someone on a personal level has never enticed me. Maybe that means something is wrong with me, but why fix what I don't feel is broken? I like myself the way I am. I just…needed more.

Edging my way down the hallway past the first two rooms, my pulse quickens as I near door number three. It's comforting that they give me the same room each time. It makes me feel…normal. Like I belong here. Like nothing is wrong with me. When I realized what kind of establishment was on the business card he slipped me, I remember I scoffed at Rory as if to say, *you've got me all wrong*. He just waltzed away with a knowing smirk, though, leaving me with that hot penny in my hand and no way to refute his assumption. Never thought I'd be so glad I didn't discard it like I had planned to.

Wiping my hand on my khakis, I reach for the doorknob, appreciating how even my skin looks blue underneath the light. I blend in with my surroundings—my peach flesh not contrasting with the black tufted wall panels. Whoever designed this place thought of everything.

You need this, Charlie, I remind myself at my moment of hesitation. Is it really hesitation, though?

It's taking everything in me to hold back from bursting into the room at the prospect of a new man behind the partition. A new mouth. New tactics of oral pleasure. The blissful release of all my stress without any complications. I can't fucking wait. The unknown is my weakness.

Pushing through the door, I step inside the little room, where I'm treated to the same soft glow of blue light as in the hallway, but much dimmer. More shadows. More intimate. Just the way I like it.

When my eyes adjust, I immediately identify the opening of my choice—the perfect height for my stature. I was apprehensive at first about how big the portals are. I always imagined they'd be just big enough to stick a cock through, but my wariness fell to the wayside upon my first visit. No one reached through the space that's large enough for a hand to fit. The large diameter of the opening afforded me the opportunity to feel whiskers and hot breath, heightening the experience.

Sliding the small round door up over the opening, I exhale and undo my fly with shaky fingers, waiting for my night's partner. I'm already half hard from the anticipation.

'*Someone new,*' the doorman said. Does that mean I had the same person for my first two visits?

I could be wrong, but I thought the technique and feel of their mouth was different each time. Perhaps he meant someone new to Illusion. I didn't come here for someone as nervous as I was on my first visit. I'll be sorely disappointed if it's someone too skittish to put their full effort into it.

The soft click of a door closing on the other side of the thin, tufted wall panel sets my ears to attention. He's here.

It's strange what you can sense just from spatial recognition. The soft approach of footsteps. The presence of a body kneeling before the other side of the opening. The proximity of another human being just on the other side of this half-inch-thick paneling. It's rigid, clearly reinforced by something inside, not giving way when I reach up and rest a hand on it above my head.

Breath in my throat, I feel a shiver at the presence of warm breath on the other side of the opening. He's ready. That's my cue.

Leaning my hips forward, I guide my tip through the opening and into the unknown. I nearly couldn't do it the first time, too afraid something would chop my dick off or bite it, but now I revel in the thrill of the eerie sensation of terror. It seems to add to the experience.

I wait. And I wait, but nothing happens.

He's there. I can tell. I can feel his breath on my tip.

Does he not like what he sees? It's difficult to see much in these darkened rooms. Did he change his mind? Is he a nervous newbie?

My disappointment flares. I've waited for this for three weeks, having been stuck on the road, traveling for work for nearly the past month. And now, I'm going to be left high and dry?

A gust of hot breath floods over my tip like a heady exhale, making me shudder. And then I feel it—a mouth. But he doesn't take me in. His lips aren't even parted. Fingertips alight on the side of my cock, making me flinch.

No one here has ever touched me with anything other than their mouth before. Granted, I knew the holes were large enough that someone could, but I suspected it was just for the illusion that it was possible, hence the name of the club.

He doesn't grab me, though, but rather just holds me in place as his closed mouth slides across my tip. I can feel moisture, but it's not from him. His lips are closed. My precum glides along the seam of his mouth, slowly, from end to end until I reach the other side of his… smile. He's smiling.

My heart kicks like a mule in my chest from the jolt that gives me all the way from my nuts. I hear a soft sound, almost like a sigh of delight. And then…his cheek brushes against my length.

It's the most surreal sensation I've ever felt. Part of me wants to shout, asking him when he's going to get to it. I don't come here for foreplay. I didn't fist and blow my way in the dark throughout college with the guy down the hall for foreplay. We did it because we both just wanted to get off discreetly in our hetero-filled frat house. This is the closest thing to that convenient accommodation that I've found since then. I don't like how the overwhelming swirl of my stomach makes me feel from this…exploration. Maybe I'm hearing things, but I swear the word, *Perfect*,' is whispered through the opening just before warm heat envelops my tip, making me feel dizzy.

Fuuuck.

It's the barest of touches, like someone slowly slurping the drippage from an ice cream cone, but it's nirvana. The peculiar smile-basting hello he gave me makes sense now. The man behind the wall definitely knows what he's doing, teasing my senses to fatten me up for the big climax. Something tells me I'm in for the ride of my life, and we've barely started.

The next thing I know, I'm engulfed in a deluge of warm heat all the way to my groin. It steals my breath and has me pressing my pelvis flush against the wall to give him everything he so eagerly took.

On my last two visits, I got a few introductory licks. The kind you give to lubricate for smooth sailing, and then the guys went to town. I definitely enjoyed myself. I came in no time, but now I can see how mechanical it all was. The fast-mouth fucking, like each guy had something to prove by how quick he could get a stranger off. Either that or they were just eager to give a blow job.

As my cock vibrates near the back of *Mystery Man Number Three's* throat, I can tell he's eager too, but not in the same way as the others. He's…all in. Holy hell, is he all in. And I definitely am too, realizing those vibrations were caused by a low, sultry groan around my cock.

Shit. That's what I want. Maybe it's what I've always wanted and just didn't know it—to feel like my cock was a hot commodity. Because let's face it, that doesn't exist in the real world without complications. Complications being relationships, neediness, tolerating another human being's poor qualities just for brief moments of pleasure that become fewer and farther between the longer you're together. I work too much to keep someone happy, and I've never actually dated a man, so I'm not going to pretend I have the first clue how. Watching my parents play a tiresome game of trying to please each other for years was enough of a preview to let me know I'm *not* a relationship guy.

Retreating slowly, his tongue spirals around me and then flicks tortuously slowly underneath my slit. He leaves me, and a pang of misery hits me over the thought of him stopping. I can still feel his heat, though. He's still there.

Skin connects with mine. It's…his hand, and it's damp. He must have licked it.

The tight draw he makes down my shaft as he suckles my tip has me gasping. I let out a high-pitched noise, which makes my face heat.

I'm a master at keeping quiet. I've had to be for most of the times I've messed around. Growing up with three very straight brothers and keeping the familial tradition of pledging to the same frat in college didn't leave me much room for openness. By the time I was out on my own in the world, where I could hook up with someone in a club or off an app, I was so used to not making a sound, it became second nature to me.

The air kisses my dick and his hand lifts it, pointing it upward, momentarily discombobulating me. A gust of hot breath wafts against my balls, reminding me how far I've leaned against the panel. Something wet against my tender flesh there gives me a start until I realize it's his tongue. And now his…mouth. I don't know why I thought a gloryhole would be smaller, just enough to allow a dick through, but I'm grateful I was wrong.

"Aw, fuck!"

He's got me *in* his mouth. His tongue swirls around one side of my sac, turning every inch of me to gooseflesh. He doesn't stop there. Tracing figure eights around each of my testicles, working into every nook and cranny, his hand works in tandem, stroking me. It swirls over my tip, gathering more of the embarrassing amount of fluids I'm leaking, using them to slather me up with each new pass.

Holy shit! He...nipped me. He fucking nipped my sac skin!

It didn't hurt exactly, but...but what the fuck? There's a sense of disorientation, but also an odd wash of heat from that peculiar act. Before I can decide if I want to draw back in case he thinks about doing it again, his mouth plunges back down my length.

The perfect amount of suction, the heat, the rhythm... The way his fingertips are now gently stroking little circles around my sack and the soft flesh at my groin like he's reminding me he wants it all—the complete package—well, it's sensory overload.

I lean my face fully into the panel, completely plastered to it now, like one of those sticky slime hands my nephews used to slap against a wall. His palm hugs my entire sac while his mouth works its slow, deliberate magic. My knees are shaking at the sensation of him cradling and giving little hugs to my jewels while his mouth does something I didn't know was possible. I can feel this orgasm building from all the way down in my pinkie toes. It's like the longest fuse ever created. I'm sweating. It's the middle of January and I'm freaking sweating.

"Shit. Aw, shit. Shit..."

He doesn't even flinch. That wicked dance of his mouth never falters. The last guy coughed halfway through, and I felt half of my release drip on the other side of the panel. The one before him, I think, moved back, so when I came, it probably painted his face.

This...this is checking boxes I didn't even know I had. It's a map of self-discovery. Everything this man has done tonight has let me in on styles of pleasure I didn't know I craved. Each pulse I make is timed perfectly with his swallows. And, fuck, I think he just moaned again. The thought of his talented mouth moaning for every drop of me after what it just did is better than any performance award I've ever earned.

A little shockwave ripples up my cock and then to my nuts. My entire body jolts from the pleasure overload. I can barely open my eyes, panting so hard my open mouth is half-squished against this panel. He's...

Aw, shit! He did it again.

He's…sucking on my tip—my flaccid tip. It's even better than the blowjob.

Unintelligible sounds tear out of my throat on each full-body tremor, each time he suckles my tip, cupping it with his tongue. It's madness. It's freaking madness. I might black out, or…or…

Shit, I'm freaking drooling. Clawing at the panel with my fingertips, it's all I can do to remain on my feet as he worships my sensitized cockhead like he doesn't want to say goodbye. I'm so out of my mind, I barely realize he's given me a reprieve until I hear a soft *thump*.

The door.

He's…gone. He left.

I'm too beautifully sated to be disappointed, but still, something inside me caves and collapses. That was life-changing. Shaking my head, I scoff at myself as I manage to peel myself off the wall and tuck myself away. *Life-changing*—that sounds so sophomoric, but truly, I don't know what else to call it. It was damn good, I guess.

I have to shake my hands out and catch my breath even after I'm put back together, before I can think of leaving the room. My legs are like spent noodles. I feel like I've been exorcised, lighter, a new man. All the planning meetings I have coming up next week don't seem as daunting now. This was definitely what I needed.

This is what I've needed for a long time.

Walking back down the hallway toward the exit, my steps feel like they're on clouds. Will he be back? I have yet to be paired with the same person each time I've been here. The dread that fills me is a crash to my high. I don't think I want to go back to unskilled performers after tonight's experience.

Stopping in the vestibule, I wait for the doorman to finish typing something on his phone. When he finally glances over at me, he raises his brows expectantly.

"The '*new one*'…" I gesture back toward the hallway with my chin, casually. "Will, uh, he be back?"

Shrugging, he glances back at his phone. "We never know."

Fuck.

Some part of me scolds myself that it doesn't matter. I can still come here to get off when I get to the point where I need more than myself to get off. Maybe the first two times were just a fluke. Maybe everyone after this guy tonight will be just as talented.

I don't realize I'm still lingering until I hear the doorman again. "Couldn't say even if I did," he informs me with a smug smirk, like he can tell how much I enjoyed myself.

The prick. I wonder if he ever partakes in the establishment's *'entertainment.'* When a jealous shard stabs me over the thought of that man lavishing him the way he just did to me, I know it's time to leave.

What the fuck do I care? It's not like I need one specific person to give me pleasure. In fact, just the opposite has always been my thing. That's why I started coming here.

Maybe I won't be back for a while this time. It's not like I'm not needy or anything.

CHAPTER 2

The following Friday

This week was brutal. Twelve-hour days. Phone calls every damn night. I must have put two thousand miles on my car. Granted, it's the company's car, but the people up at corporate probably give little thought to how much time an ass in a seat can drain a man.

Amor. What a joke that I work for a chocolatier company named *Amor* and feel little love, except for my paycheck.

Tugging the zipper of my leather jacket higher against the cold, I take swift steps across the parking lot of Illusion. I know it's only been a week since I've been here, but I'm headed to Sacramento first thing Monday morning to work my circuit there. There are only a few more weeks until Valentine's Day, our biggest sales holiday. I'm going to sink this one in the bag this year. I want it to be my best sales quarter yet. My division is going to smoke all the others—I know it. Despite my exhaustion and mental burnout, it brings me a satisfied smile. Call me competitive. Whatever. It's what I do. It's all I have to do, even as much as I bitch about it sometimes. The only hang-up is…*this.* Sometimes a guy needs to blow off some steam.

Wrapping on the door, the privacy window slides open after a few seconds. This guy is slow on purpose, I swear. I tell him the codeword, and a moment later the door opens.

I don't understand why he makes me show him my freaking ID each time. Does he think I have a twin brother?

When he checks his list to ensure that I've messaged ahead of time to reserve a spot and sent proof of my clear bill of health, he finally hands my ID back over.

"Back so soon? Liked your session last time that much, did you?"

I refuse to engage, refuse to ask him any questions. I'm realizing it's a game he plays. My pulse is kicking with an answer, all right, and maybe he can tell given that amused twinkle in his eyes. I remind myself that when Wednesday night rolled around, I didn't feel like talking myself out of coming back any longer. Only half a week before I'd caved and scheduled this visit. That's a record for me. It has nothing to do with my session last time. Nothing at all. This is about being overworked.

It doesn't matter who they send back there tonight, anyway. I've already accepted that it won't be that amazing guy from last week. That's not how these places work, is it?

I don't care. I just need to get off and am in one of those moods where it'll feel better if someone else does it for me rather than myself. I need to go to Sacramento with a clear head and a low stress meter if I want to clinch breaking my sales record.

"Room ready, or do I need to head to the lounge?" I ask, trying to sound unconcerned.

Smiling, he leans over from his stool and opens the door that leads to the private rooms. "Head on back. I'll make the call."

Waltzing through like I'm not in a hurry, like my heart rate isn't accelerated, I head down the hallway. After a few steps, I realize he didn't tell me which room number. I've always been in number three. Glancing to my left, the first two rooms have the red bar of occupancy showing on the locking mechanism. Maybe they give returning visitors the same room each time.

The slider on door number three is green. Oddly, it makes me feel a sense of coming home, or at the very least, welcome. How did a club that features glory holes ever become a place of normalcy for me? The anticipation and the unnerving hope that I'll be treated the way I was last time have me brushing the question from my mind as I enter the room.

Adjusting my eyes to the dark blue lighting, I zero in on the cover of the opening I prefer and unzip my jacket. Zipper halfway down, I stop.

It's open. The cover is already open.

Odd.

Hanging my jacket on the hook by the door, I keep my eye on the darkened circle as I undo my fly. I hope to hell they didn't forget to clean the thing after the last pair left. Unless…

Unless you can open them from either side and…

Swallowing, I step up to the tufted paneling and swear I sense movement on the other side. It's so damn difficult to detect any sign of shadows with the blue lighting in here. That familiar fear mixed with excitement courses through me as I angle the head of my cock to breach the opening.

This is the worst part—the waiting. Those initial seconds when your cock is exposed through the portal, unaware of what awaits you. And yet, it makes everything after the best part. When your fear is crested by pleasure. Your bravery, rewarded by desire.

A breath…slow and hot breath dusts my exposed flesh. I shudder instantly.

It's *him*. I know it is.

Any remaining doubt is erased when the faintest of kisses touches down on my tip. It's featherlight. It's innocent. It's almost nothing, but it makes my breath stutter, like I'm going through hypothermia.

"Yes," I whisper, thanking any higher being for this good fortune.

I feel his hand next. Gently, it palms the side of my shaft, steadying it. For what, I'm unsure, until soft stubble presses against the other side. A cheek. A jawline.

It's like how a cat rubs seductively against someone's leg. I can feel the curve of his earlobe, a lock of soft hair. His lips press against the warm skin of my groin, right next to my root. A delirious puff of air leaves my mouth, piecing the act together. It's like he's honoring me from tip to base with that bit of reverence. Saying grace before he has his meal.

I am so fucking glad I booked this tonight.

The bass of the music from the lounge oozes through the walls, making it difficult to discern noises, but I swear he just inhaled. Inhaling my scent is an instant addition to my new list of boxes that like being checked.

Shifting, he trails his cheek slowly back down my length. His warm breath coats me the entire way until his lips turn and capture my tip. Softly. Slowly. Delicately. It's a fucking art what this guy does.

Burying my forehead in my forearm against the wall, I shift as carefully as I can, not wanting to disturb any of his plans. I inch my hips forward, pressing them flush against the panel, so he'll have as much access to as much of me as I can give him. My balls are all the way through the opening now. It's nothing short of pleading for him to repeat what he did last time. I want it all. Whatever tricks he has up his sleeve, I want to find out.

His thumb circles over my tip. I don't even care that I'm leaking already when I feel him smear my precum around and plant a soft kiss on each side of my sac. His tongue gives me a start when I feel it flick the underside of my balls. It's so close to my taint—a first for me.

The only person who's ever played with my ass is me. It's just…not my thing. I'm very certain someone else playing with it probably wouldn't be my thing, but his proximity is surprisingly acceptable at the moment.

It's like we have chemistry. I know that sounds ludicrous, but I can't explain it any other way. It's not just the unknown or the thrill of secrecy. We have this surreal physical compatibility.

He proves my theory correct, working his deliberate magic on me like he did last time, but with new moves and more fervor. The slow, torturous teasing. The artful caressing. His fingers circle around my balls at one point and cinch them, giving me a sense of alarm and confusion at first. But then the way he ravages my cock while he holds me soon lets me know he's prolonging my release. It's shocking and terrifying over how possessive it feels, but also…fucking amazing. I'm about to pass out from the level of need for release.

"Please… please. Oh, please." I can't believe I'm chanting such wanton words into this wall.

I don't know if he heard me, but he releases my jewels just when I think I can't take anymore, and I spill down his throat. It's even more euphoric than last time—the succession of pulse, swallow, pulse, swallow. He's a riverbed and I'm the mighty river flowing. There are tears in my eyes over how magnificent I feel. The man deserves a medal.

With each little suckle of my flaccid tip sending tremors through me, I whine deliriously, clawing at the wall. I'm going to end up a puddle on the floor. That mouth—that mouth of his…

The sweet, reverent suction is my undoing. I need…to be closer to it. Need to thank him for this gift he's given me a second time. Without thinking, my hand goes to the portal.

Hesitantly, I slip my index and middle fingers through the hole. I don't want to scare him off, but he needs to know how much I appreciate his talents.

Did *he* get off? I don't think I felt him jostling at all, jerking himself. How can he give so much and take so little in return?

It's not like I can wave to him or say thank you, so I just hook my fingers through the portal, offering another form of my presence. A way to pay him homage.

His mouth leaves my tip, and the next thing I know, his damp warmth covers my fingertips. I'm treated to that same delicate suction on each of them. Then he swirls his tongue around both of my digits.

No one's ever sucked on my fingers. I've never even thought of having that done to me. Moaning like they're a second cock I didn't know I had, I glance down in awe even though I can't see what he's doing.

I get a soft kiss on my knuckles and realize it's over. It can't be over. I know it has to be, but...

In a panic, I drop to a knee. "Next week?" I ask softly, urgently. "Please tell me you'll be here next week."

I can double down on my Sacramento trip and be back by Friday afternoon. I need this. I need more of him, or at least to make some kind of arrangement. After this, no one else here is going to compare to this man.

Squinting in the silence, I wonder if he's gone. If he headed to the door already and didn't hear me. I can feel tension in the air, though, and then I see movement. It's just shadows, but I can make out his lower jaw and a hint of his dark stubble.

Have I ruined it? The club has rules. There's a waiver you have to agree to when you schedule a session, and a sign in each room listing all the rules.

No talking.

No soliciting.

No breaching the barrier.

I've done all three, but I can't help it. He's quiet. Will he report me? The waiver says there are strict repercussions for breaking the rules. I assume that means being banned, but what the hell do I care about being banned if it won't be him next time? How can I go back to anything else after experiencing *him*?

"You're...incredible," I confess, a last-ditch effort to reassure him I only have good intentions.

Mouth parted, he hovers. He's still there, at least. It means he's considering it. Will he turn me down?

I wait, suspended in my worry. And then...his lips move.

It's just a whisper, a low, smooth whisper, but I've never heard better words. "Next week."

CHAPTER 3

Fucking finally. The swiftness of my steps, taking me to the back door of Illusion, is like walking on air.

I did it. I topped my all-time sales record and even managed to score two new accounts on my trip this week. It was a feat driven by sheer determination to be home before Friday. I've well-beyond qualified for the new private cruise incentive the company is awarding to the top salespeople from each region, but I couldn't care less at the moment. There's only one thing on my mind.

The doorman's quirky greeting and tedious verification process don't even faze me this time. As soon as I push through the hallway door to the private rooms, my heart is fluttering.

He said he'd be here. I hope to hell he didn't change his mind.

Once inside my room, my fingers fumble with my jacket zipper, trembling as I spy the open portal. It was open the last time, too, because he arrived before I did. Does that mean he's here already?

The thought of him being as eager as I am has me breathing fast and heavy, my cock thickening even more than the wood I've been sporting all week. Unfastening my jeans, I let out a sigh of relief, freeing myself from the constraints of the denim. I can smell my shower gel even through the potent aroma of the leather-upholstered paneling.

Will he notice I trimmed things up down there? I don't know why I'm bothering to wonder. It's not like I've ever taken the time to go an extra mile in the prep department for a guy before. I just figured being…extra clean was the polite thing to do since he agreed to meet me again. It's not like there are many ways to repay him.

Swallowing against the thick lump in my throat, I angle my tip through the darkened hole. My skin is prickled in gooseflesh. Like always, the fear is still there, but this time, it's the fear of being disappointed.

The portal was open already, Charlie. Just like he opened it last time. It's him. Don't worry.

Hot breath kisses my skin. A fingertip traces a gentle line up the underside of my shaft from base to tip. It *is* him. I know it.

Sighing, I lean into the panel with a dopey smile on my face, all my worry fading away. When his stubble brushes against my cock as he places a soft kiss to my navel, every bit of tension from the week vanishes. The man is like a full-body sedative.

He begins his slow, teasing preview. Open-mouthed glides down the side of my cock. Little flicks of the tip of his tongue. Butterfly kisses that should not be a fucking turn on but have me sinking into a thick fog of lust. *He* is my incentive award. *This.* I'm going to dream about every second of tonight when I'm stuck on that stupid cruise.

When he finally does that suckling thing to my tip, I tense briefly at the feel of his palm on my balls. He's…cupping them. Massaging them.

Why did I even question it? Like every other experience with him thus far, it feels fantastic.

Pressing my hips against the panel as tightly as I can, I give him a silent sign of my approval. It's like saying *don't stop* without having to voice those needy words. My face heats remembering how I whispered to him last time, *'You're incredible.'*

I don't do pillow talk. Never have. I've never needed to. Everything with my old college dorm mate was concise and instructional—*'yeah, like that.'* And I've certainly never uttered anything like praise to the few casual hook-ups I've had since then.

This is better—this silent meeting of like minds. Now that he agreed to return, I'll never have to flail myself like a starry-eyed teen again. Clearly, the man knows what I need and is happy to give it.

His mouth envelops me all the way to the back of his throat, pulling a groan from mine in response. He goes to town, working his talents in tight, warm, wet pulls of his magical mouth. The pressure on my balls increases, and my foggy brain tries to picture every action that's possibly happening on the other side of the wall to bring me such bliss.

He's clenching his fingers around my sac again, just like last time, but tighter. It's familiar to me now, so I don't feel any apprehension, even if it's more intense. The speed and confines of his mouth, however, are definitely proof that he's brought his A-game tonight, driving me madder than ever.

Grinding my teeth, I groan and dig my fingertips into the panel. I want to rock my hips so badly, but don't dare move so as not to disrupt his plan. It's odd how much trust this requires when I'm not a trusting person. It's almost liberating to let go for a change. Maybe that's the appeal.

I don't know what's more intense as he mounts a full-scale attack on my sanity; the pressure in my cock or around my balls. I'd come any second if he'd release his hold on my nuts, but his grip doesn't budge. In fact, it's getting tighter. It almost feels like… something else is there. Something…rubbery. Like the texture of one of my silicone kitchen spatulas. Something metal brushes the underside of my cock at my base.

Does he…have a wedding ring? Picturing one on his finger pierces my heart. There's no earthly reason why that should disappoint me. I have no opinion on infidelity.

Why should I? I don't do relationships.

Still…it's odd to think he belongs to someone else. To *someone*, I mean. Odd to think he belongs to *someone* while he's doing *this* to *me*.

I'm about to cry out and beg for him to release his hold on my sac, to tell him he's successfully driven me to enough of a euphoric withholding, when my body racks in a violent shudder. It's almost painful the way my orgasm rips through me against the constraint until it's not. It's fucking heaven.

I couldn't open my eyes if I tried. My head is swimming in a haze of blackness while it feels like a life force is being drained out of my cock as I pulse into that wicked mouth of his.

It's taking everything in me to keep myself on my feet. Fingers digging into the wall, I cling to it to hold me up as I moan and whimper like some distraught creature. I'm numb and weightless. How can I be weightless and yet feel so heavy? I never knew orgasms could feel like this.

He does that reverent, delicate suction to my tip in the aftermath, like he's thanking it, making a tear track down my cheek. My entire body is trembling with little shudders from the sensory overload. My sensitized cock. The still-drawn-up feeling in my balls, even though I've spent more than I think I ever have.

I twitch when something touches my cock again. More metal.

Fuck. I do not need to feel that wedding ring again right now.

Just let me enjoy the comedown, I want to tell him.

Except it feels like it's everywhere as his fingers move around my flaccid cock. Hard, steely metal. Thick, round bands of it. It's not on his finger. I can feel his fingers gently pinching my base like he's…directing me inside of…*something*.

My dormant dick rests on a bed of something spinelike, cold and metallic. Did he…put something…*on* my cock?

Suspended in confusion, I don't dare move a muscle. As my haze clears, it's evident there's still something cinching my balls tight. A light force jostles me, almost like something clicking shut, but…on my cock. His hold on my balls finally relinquishes. I can't feel his skin there anymore, except…*something* is still there. Something wrapped tightly around the circumference of my nuts. A band, that silicone sensation I thought I felt earlier.

I…

He…

Did he just put…a cock cage on me?

A bizarre wave floods through me. It's a strange mix of arousal and terror. I've never even seen a cock cage. Pictures in porn, sure. But that's where they belong—in porn. They're certainly nothing I'd ever dabble in. I mean, it basically means someone owns your dick, right?

There's that odd tremor again. What the fuck is up with me?

I must still be coming down from my orgasm because there's no way someone owning my dick would turn me on. Maybe through this glory hole for fifteen minutes, but via a cock cage? Not a chance.

Steadying my breathing, I wait.

Patience, Charlie. He's not let you down once yet. Maybe this is just one more means of pleasure he has up his sleeve.

Maybe he just wants to give me the sensation of being restrained for a few minutes, and he's going to take it off for a second round. A round two would be worth tolerating this unexpected device for a few moments.

God, it feels strange. So snug, almost like I'm wearing a watch, but…not.

The damndest thing of all is I can feel myself getting turned on again already. I nearly blacked out from what he just put me through. How in the hell am I going to survive it twice? I suppress a delirious laugh at the thought of having to crawl out of Illusion to get to my car, so drained from pleasure that I can't use my legs.

A light draft chills my exposed skin from the other side of the panel. There's a soft click, but this time, it isn't on my cock. The wall vibrated when it happened.

No…

Did he just walk out the door?

It feels like minutes, but it's probably only seconds as I stand rigid with terror. I can't just wait here if he's actually left.

Why would he leave? Did he need to use the bathroom?

Surely, he'll come back. He wouldn't just leave me like this. That would be cruel. He's not cruel. He's…

He's…

What am I saying? I don't know a thing about him.

Every pleasant feeling that was left in me is snuffed out like a candle flame. It's like a blanket of my own stupidity settles over me, leaving a nauseous sensation in my stomach. The reality is suddenly vivid. I trusted a total stranger with my dick in a precarious manner.

Fuck!

Gingerly, I inch back from the wall, imagining the worst. Being chained to the other side is one possibility. How the fuck do I know what this guy did to me?

The blue lighting reveals my flesh, however, showing me that some type of band is indeed cinched around my balls. What follows next makes my breath catch. Metal bands, braced by another thin one that connects them all the way down to my tip. It *is* a fucking cock cage.

"Fuck. Are you fucking kidding me?"

Tugging at the end of it pulls the flesh around my sac and navel, causing discomfort. Shit. I'll need to unfasten it, but I can't see the fine details of the contraption in this crap lighting. I don't see any kind of release mechanism on the band that's cinching me, holding me hostage to the cage.

Hostage. My cock is *not* a hostage.

Fucking hell. Why would he do this? I don't understand.

If he wasn't enjoying this, he could have just declined last time. Does fucking someone over turn him on?

I can't believe he hasn't come back. This has to just be a messed-up joke.

The only other person here that I've talked to is the dickhead doorman. Great. Fucking great.

Is *that* the joke? Slap one of these on a guy, so he has to go out there and beg for help from that jerk? No fucking way.

There has to be a way to get these things off by yourself. Otherwise, people wouldn't wear them, right?

One thing is clear—standing in here isn't the answer to my problem. Tucking myself away, I wince, trying to angle my captured nuts back into my jeans. This is *so* not funny. You can see a fucking indent on my fly from the cage. It looks like I'm sporting a damn semi.

Stepping out into the hallway, I glance toward the door to the vestibule. The coast is clear; not that anyone might notice the secret in my pants in this shadowed corridor.

With each step, my junk shifts, something it's always done, but it never felt like this. It is incredibly obvious to my conscience that I'm wearing a…device. I've never been more hyper-aware of my body. It's so…strange. If I wasn't freaking the fuck out, it might feel sexual in a pleasant way like it did for a moment back in that room. Right now, though, it's a fucking time bomb. This freaking doorman better have good news for me.

"Hey," I call as I push through the door to the vestibule, hooking my thumb into the waist of my jeans so my hand can cover part of my fly. "Is…number three still here? He just up and left."

After five annoyingly long seconds, he finally looks at me and hikes his brows. "Maybe he didn't like what he saw."

Fuck him. This fucking fuck.

"Hilarious. Pretty sure he was the same guy as last week, so I doubt it, but…"

"But what?"

What do I say? I'm sure as shit not showing this asshole the state of my dick right now, let alone admitting to him my predicament.

"I…I need to talk to him."

"No talking to the visitors. It's in the rules," he drawls, tapping the sign behind him with his pen before looking back at some video of funny dog antics on his phone.

"I know that. I do, but is he still here? Did you see him leave? I just…need to know if he's coming back to the room. We weren't…finished."

"Left you high and dry, did he?" He smirks, glancing down at my fly. I don't know whether he can tell what I'm concealing or if he just looked because he's a fucking pain in the ass who enjoys messing with me. "That'll happen sometimes. Visitors' choice. That's one rule we don't make."

"No. He just…" Fuck. This is going to be either humiliating or a waste of my time. I already know it. "He…did something to me."

Frowning, he looks up from his stupid video. "Did he break the rules?"

"What? No. No, he just…"

"If there were no club violations, there's nothing I can do."

I'm going to get nowhere with this guy. This is bullshit. How could that guy do this to me after…after we did…*things*?

"Look, I know you'll probably say this is some club violation, but do me a favor. If you see him again, give him my card," I tell him, yanking one out of my wallet and handing it to him.

He blinks at it without moving like the worthless, stubborn pile of meat he is. "Please," I urge, thrusting it closer to him. "I'm not a stalker. I can't call him unless he calls me this way, right?"

Narrowing his eyes at me, he asks, "What's it worth to you?"

Un-fucking-real. So, the rules can be broken as long as you pay up. I see how it is.

I flip through my money and pull out three one-hundred-dollar bills. That should let him know I mean business.

His expression doesn't even change, but he takes the money along with my card. I watch with bated breath as he tucks both into the pocket of his leather vest. And then…he fucking picks up his phone and starts watching his stupid dog videos again.

"Does that mean you'll give it to him?"

A beat. And then a shrug. "Maybe."

I have to bite my tongue to hold back all the expletives I want to call him. Stowing my wallet, I shove out the door into the parking lot before I lose my shit.

"Fuck!" I yell into the night.

A couple nearly slams into me, looking taken aback by my outburst. Shit. I didn't even see them. Both blond, with no facial hair—the first thing that comes to mind is that neither of them is *him*. All I know is that he has dark stubble. There's no way I could identify him, even if he walked right past me.

Fuck him. I don't need him to get this thing off me.

"Sorry. Excuse me," I mumble and head to my car, walking like a cowboy that's been in the saddle for too long.

How do people even wear these? It certainly can't be for very long, and definitely won't be so in my case. As soon as I get home, I'm getting myself free.

A fucking sex club. What in the ever-loving hell was I thinking?

CHAPTER 4

"I can't fucking believe this." I kill my car's engine and glare across the parking lot at the black door that got me into this mess. I never should have set foot in this damn place.

It's Tuesday night, and my junk is *still* locked up like Fort Knox. If I ever find that guy, I'm going to kick his ass. Then, when he recuperates, I'm going to kick it again.

Nothing has worked. I did a deep dive on the internet like any educated American, and I can tell you one thing—all the posts from people saying you can slide these fuckers off by yourself, haven't had once cinched as tight around their nuts as this one. It's a freaking thick-ass cable, coated in silicone. I know this because after I snipped through a section of the silicone, I discovered the industrial-looking cable beneath. Trying to snip at a thick ass cable pressed tight up against your most delicate areas is something I never want to attempt again. I didn't nick myself, but it was obvious that would be the result.

I saw a video once of a woman who went to the ER when her finger swelled up. They had to cut her ring off with a grinding wheel. So, yeah, the fucking ER is out too.

Folding my dick out through the base of the cage was one more useless piece of advice from the self-proclaimed experts online. There are only a few centimeters between the first steel ring of the cage and this stupid cable. God, that guy must be twisted. He found the mother of all devices. *In-fucking-escapable.*

Seriously. There's no escape.

The end of the stupid cable he cinched me up with runs through a hollow opening of the spine of the cage and connects with a locking device on the first ring. A *numerical* locking device. Who puts a numerical lock on a sex device? That should be illegal.

Four numbers. That's all I need is four numbers. My back is killing me from sitting hunched over for so long over the last few days, trying to break the code. I swear by all that's holy, I tried every damn combination of numbers possible, but no dice. I can't freaking call in sick another day.

I mean, technically, I can, but fuck that. I'm not burning my leave for time I can't enjoy. And I have shit to get done before I leave for the cruise on Friday morning.

Getting out of my car, I stride toward the dreaded door of Illusion. I take no pride in the fact I've learned to walk more normally now with my new attachment. As long as I ignore how it feels like someone is cupping my testicles and dick, I have no reason to divert from my usual stride.

If I was certain I could get this thing off me in time for the damn work cruise, I wouldn't even be here. My boss, Colin, can suck my imprisoned cock for the news he dropped on me today. I emailed to inform him I was going to pass on the cruise. I assumed he'd tell me, *'Sure. No problem.'* I never expected my phone to ring with a warning that I might want to rethink my decision.

'Charlie, you don't want to miss it. They're going to restructure marketing from operations and want to hire a VP of marketing at the corporate office. That's what the cruise is for. Corporate wants to get to know the top salespeople in the company on a personal level and hand-pick who they want to offer the position to. You didn't hear that from me, though.'

Of all the weeks Colin's connections with corporate proved useful, it had to be *this* one. Maybe I'd have been less pissed off if I'd found out after the fact that I missed out on a huge career advancement. Now that I know, however, like hell am I going to let anyone I outsold get that promotion over me. Less travel. More money. *A lot* more money. That job is mine.

I just need to fucking lose the worst practical joke ever played in history. Right after I put up with the dickhead at the door.

"ID," he says, giving me a chin nod.

I can't with him tonight.

"Are you fucking serious? I've been here how many times now, and I know you certainly remember me from last time." I chin nod right back, directing my eyes to his vest pocket. The prick.

Folding his burly arms across his chest, he inhales, increasing his size by a few inches. "Mind your tone, please, sir. This is a respectable establishment."

My ass it is! Biting the inside of my lip, I yank my wallet out of my pocket, vibrating with anger. If he kicks me out, I won't get my chance to see if this is my saving grace.

For all I know, the three hundred bucks I gave him last week might actually pay off. Maybe he made sure to call my room partner for my session tonight. I know it's supposedly against their stupid rules, but I even put it in my notes when I scheduled online.

Prefer same partner as last time.

I'm not even going to ask him. That's what he wants. This guy is all about looking superior. I bet that's why he's giving me shit right now. No doubt, he wants me to grovel before I can go back there and find out if he put my money to good use.

Oddly, that puts me at ease as the dickhead finally returns my ID. I have no idea what will transpire once I get back to the room, but, surely, the man in number three will take this damn thing off me. You can't look your crime in the face and ignore it.

Making my way down the hallway, I resent the quickening of my pulse. It's like I've been conditioned to think pleasure awaits at the end of the hall. It sure as shit didn't end in pleasure the last time. Opening the door to my room, I hate the mix of arousal and dread in my belly.

Neither should be there. I wouldn't let this guy pleasure me again even if he begged, and I shouldn't be living in fear that one man's presence holds the fate of my cock.

I stop dead in my tracks when my eyes adjust to the darker light in the room. The portal—the one I've always used—is closed. Shit.

It is Tuesday, after all. I've only been here on Fridays. More importantly, as far as I know, *he's* only been here on Fridays. My three hundred bucks had to have bought me something. Even though the doorman is a pain in the ass, I know it's just a game. He wouldn't do me dirty like this. Would he?

Maybe the guy isn't in his side of the room yet. Maybe he wants to mess with me some more and make me wait.

Fuck it. What other options do I have short of risking a fatal injury if I go at it with the wire snippers again? I want this thing off me, so my head is clear for the work trip of a lifetime.

Blowing out a breath, I lower my fly. How absurd is it that the sight of this contraption is starting to seem familiar to me? Like it's a part of me. The cinch isn't exactly painful now that I've been stuck with it for four days. It's just…fucking uncomfortable and distracting as hell. It's like the entire thing makes my junk feel… perky and…on alert. Almost primed.

Shaking the thoughts away, I pinch my eyes shut for a second. Is that what the guy wanted? For me to think about being hard for him after our session? I could have told him I would have done that without this ridiculous device on me.

Opening the portal door, I wait and listen. I can't hear anything, can't sense a presence on the other side. I don't know why I think I'd feel better knowing he was there rather than no one. He's the one who got me into this, and he's clearly not trustworthy.

If he is in there, he's being as quiet as a mouse, waiting for me to show the source of my shame. The jerk. As soon as this thing is off, I'm pulling the fuck out and booking it out of here without a backward glance.

Sidling up to the wall, I hold my breath and angle my entombed dick through the opening. And then… nothing. I wait and wait, trying to convince myself that time is going by slower than I imagine. I'm about to give up and go give the doorman a piece of my mind when I hear the door on the other side. It clicks open and then shut.

Footsteps. Warmth—not warm breath like I'm used to from him, just the subtle warmth of another person's presence. The warmth gets closer, making my heart skip a beat. He must be on his knees now.

What was that noise? A scoff?

There's a sliding sound. One of the portal doors to my left opens, and a voice floats through, making me nearly jump out of my skin.

"Um…cute look you got going here, guy, but what the hell am I supposed to do with this?" It's higher-pitched and laughing.

It's…not him.

Fuck.

Oh, fuck.

CHAPTER 5

Staring at the suitcase lying open on my bed, it seems foolish to debate whether to bring swim trunks on this cruise. The welcome email I received highlighted all the amenities on the luxury yacht, including a pool and two hot tubs. There's no way I want to risk the chance of someone seeing the outline of my cage in my trunks. Yet, the thought of the cool water soothing my nuts might be a welcome relief and help get me through the necessary mingling. I can't just hide in my cabin the entire week while everyone else is living it up in the public areas. I'll look like I either don't want the job or I'm some weirdo who hibernates to jerk off. If I could jerk off right now…

Grunting, I adjust myself and toss my trunks on top of a stack of the loosest-fitting shorts I own and zip the case closed. If I weren't impeded and didn't hate that man right now, I'd get out my lube, stroke myself stupid, and pretend it was his mouth doing the job.

Is he even thinking about me, I wonder. This is so not fair. He could be out there getting laid right now. Is he enjoying the fact that I have to wait for him to get relief?

A shudder ripples through me, nearly making my knees buckle. Damn. How can I be lightheaded at the odd punch of arousal from the thought of that level of possessiveness? It's so bizarre. I'm as independent as they come. I've clearly been stuck in this thing far too long if I'm getting hot and bothered about possessiveness over my dick.

Flopping back on the bed, I throw my arm over my eyes and blow out a breath of frustration. That jackass doorman threw me out and told me not to come back when I demanded to speak to the owner. He wanted to know my complaint. I could have fessed up, but I wouldn't give him the satisfaction of discovering my predicament. Knowing him, he'd accuse me of putting it on myself or tell me what the internet said—that I can get it off on my own.

Maybe I can hire a private doctor to make a house call. One who's discreet, has incredibly steady hands, and can get access to the world's tiniest grinding tool. The thought of marred flesh at the V of my groin has my stomach churning. I could weep, I swear.

How am I supposed to get through this cruise? I can barely focus, clouded by desperation and arousal. All I can think about is my dick…and *him*. The strangest part is how sad I feel. It's a weighty sensation deep in my chest at the realization my dick has been abandoned. Someone locked it up and threw away the key, like it doesn't matter or deserve a chance. It was a good dick. It didn't deserve this.

If I could at least just get off once before I have to go to the airport in the morning, maybe I'll survive this trip without looking like I'm constipated the entire time and making a fool of myself. I'm so sensitive down there that it's starting to affect the rest of my body. My nipples have been hard nonstop. When I shampoo my hair, scrubbing my scalp feels almost erotic and has me moaning. I think this thing is making me want to be touched everywhere else since I can't do anything with my cock.

That's not entirely true, though, is it? Some of those forum articles I read said you can still get off while wearing a cage. They called it a dry release. Some described it as less than satisfying, while others said they love it when they hold a vibrator on the cage while…

Ugh. That's not going to work either. I tried prostate stimulation once in college. Once was enough to prove to me that trying to jam my finger into my ass wasn't satisfying. I went on my merry way with oral and then, after graduation, I finally worked up the nerve to fuck a guy I met at a bar. People with macho asshat brothers like mine aren't big on experimenting. I found what works for me and stuck with it nicely and discreetly until this fucking mess.

I think that's what makes this so cruel. I'm a private person. I wasn't looking for anything kinky. I wasn't harming anyone and didn't deserve to be punished. All I wanted was some relief the way I like to get relief at a place that supposedly boasts they can provide it. I think I ask for very little from the world of sex, and now I'm being tortured.

Grinding my teeth, I can't believe I'm actually contemplating prostate stimulation. I shouldn't have to, but what other option do I have? I don't even own a vibrator. Why would I? The only thing I have that vibrates is…

Ah, shit. I didn't pack my toiletries bag yet.

Shoving off the bed, I grunt at the way my over-sensitized skin feels pressed against the metal bars. In the bathroom, I cringe at the bags under my eyes in the mirror. I look exhausted, but at least I'm clean shaven. Unplugging my razor, I grab my toiletries bag and head back to my room. I don't know how in the hell I'm going to get any rest tonight, being this turned on. It'll be a miracle if I don't pass out from sleep deprivation on day one of this stupid cruise. I can't believe people on those forums I read said they actually enjoy being in these things. Maybe that's because, unlike me, they know they can get out of theirs.

I'm about to drop my electric razor into my bag when I realize for the first time just how perfectly curved it is. It's a slight angle, similar to the one on the cage.

A wave of heat floods my face over even considering it, while a fire blooms in my belly and spreads lower. My cock throbs against the cage like it's begging to make the decision for me. Some of those guys said they loved how it felt holding a vibrator against their enclosure. I would love to love anything about my predicament, even for only a few minutes.

"Fuck it," I grumble, yanking my sleep pants down and climbing onto the bed.

Oh brother, this looks strange—both the cage on my cock and the sight of my shaver in my hand next to it. I need to turn my brain off. That's the only way I'll be able to do this.

Flipping the switch, the device buzzes to life. Closing my eyes, my lungs are locked up in anticipation. Will this bring me pleasure or further discomfort?

An embarrassing sound tears from my throat the second I touch the shaver to the frame of the cage. Holy fuck. That feels good.

It's like my dick has become part of the cage, vibrating right along with the metal. Shocks course through my navel and down my thighs, making my eyes want to roll back in my head.

Moaning, I drop my free hand to the bed to brace myself. Jesus, my thighs are quivering. It's unbelievable—I think…I might actually be able to come.

I'm so hard now, my tip is pressed up against the end of the cage, nearly bulging out of the opening. It should be obscene, but the longer I blink through the sensations of rapture, the more the sight turns me on. A cock—a bulging, pressurized cock, pleading silently to come. If my nuts draw up any higher, I might pass out.

"Come. Please. Please come."

How those are words leaving my mouth, I don't understand. I never talk when I masturbate. I barely even talk when I'm with a guy.

That delicious buzzing is criminal. I can feel it all the way down to my toes like a string is connected between my cock and my appendages. I *have to* be close. I have to. I can't take the pressure much longer.

I thought it was just my thighs that were quivering, but I realize it's because I've been trying to hold still and not look like a feral animal with blue balls. I give up the fight and let my hips rock. It's so bizarre. Thrusting like I'm fucking isn't going to help me achieve release, but instinct has taken over, instinct and a week of being deprived of release and teased to the point of torment.

"Come on. Uhn. Come on," I grunt, gritting my teeth through the tightening pressure.

I can feel every centimeter of the cable around my sac, cinching my swollen flesh tighter. Its cruel message is '*no*,' while my body is screaming '*yes*.' I freaking sound like I'm winded, my heart hammering against my ribcage. All my muscles are locked up the way they usually get right before I release. I *have* to come soon. Any second now. Even my ass muscles are clenched in anticipation of the impending glory. Kneading my fingertips into one cheek, I grip a handful, hoping to alleviate at least one point of tension in my body.

My hips jerk like I have no control over them. My pucker twitches so violently, I slam my eyes shut.

Shit. My eyes just crossed from touching my ass. That's…so fucking weird. I'm not an ass guy. This has to stop before I either pass out or my nuts burst, but not in the good way. Sucking in a breath, I ease my index finger lower. I can't believe I'm even contemplating this. I know it's not going to feel good, but there's this incessant hungry need growing inside my hole. Grazing the pad of my finger between my cheeks, a loud moan falls from my lips.

"Aw, fuck. Yeah." They're hopeful words, encouraged by the jolt of bliss that charges through me at that simple touch. "Please," I add, because apparently, I don't care what comes out of my mouth anymore.

Scrambling for my nightstand drawer, I grab my bottle of lube. Fumbling it open with one hand, I don't dare release my grip on the shaver and the cage. With my luck, stopping would send me into some further kind of delayed release effect from this cage. The liquid squirts all over the damn place, dribbling down my hand and onto the sheets. If I don't get this thing off me by the time the cruise is over, I'm going right back to Illusion and waiting outside the door until they let me talk to the owner.

Finger slick, I pinch my eyes closed and try to focus on the pleasure and not the memories of discomfort this once brought me. Pressing against my ring, it's strange how hot it feels against my fingertip. It's strange how much it feels like my digit could be a thin cock. It's even more strange that there's this gnawing ache deep inside me, like it wants to feel a thin cock reach out and touch it. Blowing out a breath, I press back onto my fingertip on another animalistic thrust of my hips. Too animalistic…

"Uhn… F-fuck. Ah!"

Hot waves of breath flood from my open mouth like I've just run a sprint. I feel it. I can feel my prostate and let out a delirious sound, almost like a laugh. Vibrations in the front and heaven in the back—this is beyond surreal. I don't dare open my eyes, not that I'd be able to see what I look like locked up while impaled on my own damn finger. I'm beyond caring because I think I've finally found the secret to my success.

All I hear for the next few minutes is buzzing and unholy wanton sounds that don't sound like they belong to me. My hand is starting to cramp. I can feel a sheen of sweat on my chest and at the small of my back, but I let my body do what the urges demand. Riding and buzzing. Buzzing and riding. It's hell, and it's the edge of a bliss I might actually kill for.

"Yeah. Please! Please!"

Some part of my hazy brain comprehends the complete neediness that's taken over me. The pitiful desperation is something akin to submissiveness. There's no one here to be submissive to but the just-out-of-reach pleasure. Yet even that stoic shred of me that's still somewhere online is forgiving. The needier I sound, the more I give over, and the closer I feel to coming. The further away from my stressors. I don't know if I've ever felt this…light.

My back arches as though something's possessed me. The cage bucks in my grip. I open my eyes, but my vision is blurry as a wave of pressure rushes up through my cock and my gland spasms against my fingertip.

It's an orgasm like I've never experienced. There's a plume of pleasure in my channel that has me twitching and trying to see straight. And yet…my cock is softening like its job is done. I can feel it easing away from the end of the cage. I don't understand…

When my eyes finally focus again, I click the shaver off and let it fall from my numb hand. Precum is dribbling from the end of the cage into a small pool on my sheets. Something crippling grips the pit of my stomach and my heart. It feels…a lot like sadness.

Fuck. I'm soft. It's over.

It can't be over. That can't be all there was.

And yet, it seems like it would be greedy to want more, because that was something epic. My weak legs collapse, leaving me sitting on my heels as I stare at my entombed cock and my swollen sac. A sound pierces the silence. I ignore it the first time while my brain tries to make heads or tails of the bliss I just experienced and how it can be followed by this soul-crushing sensation of disappointment.

I weep again with more volume, and a tear tracks down my cheek. It's not disappointment that's imprisoning my emotions right now. It's…yearning.

I need…*him*.

I can't fucking explain it. Fifteen minutes ago, I would never have thought those words. Whatever trying to achieve release in this stranger's cage just did to me, however, is pummeling me with the cruelest sensation yet. If I thought I was breathing hard a moment ago, this epiphany has me damn near hyperventilating now. Because… because some foreign part of me feels like it wouldn't mind weeping and begging all night if it meant some knight would rescue me from his shining armor.

CHAPTER 6

This cruise just had to start in Hawaii. A fucking island. Of all the shit I worried about this week, I completely forgot about the process of going through airport security. The mental image of that TSA worker's expression as he looked at my body scan will haunt me for the rest of my days. Eyes pinched shut, he shook his head and waved me on like I was too big of a pervert to question. Does that mean he sees cock cages all the time or that he'd already dealt with enough weird shit for one day before I came along?

Huffing, I grimace at my reflection in my cabin's mirror. Of course, I can tell the cage is there behind my cargo shorts. The question is, will everyone else, or am I just being self-conscious? The entire flight from Seattle to Honolulu had me squirming in my seat, wondering if the smiles from the flight attendants were a mockery because of my secret. This thing has now gone beyond affecting my sex drive. It's making me paranoid.

At least Carmen and Niel, two salespeople from other regions that I linked up with at the Honolulu airport, didn't seem to notice on the drive to the harbor. Not even the overwhelming size of this superyacht when we made our way down the docks was able to make me forget my reality, though.

I was shown by the steward to my cabin without having to see anyone else, but the damn CEO of the company is supposed to be hosting this trip. Michael McDonnell—the name I've seen on emails countless times will be here in the flesh, and I'm wearing a fucking cock cage.

If I fixate on possible scenarios of my condition being outed to him and costing me this promotion, I'll never be able to focus enough to prevent such from happening. I need to keep my head in the game and treat this like a sales trip so I can work the room when it comes time to socialize. As long as I can keep everyone's eyes up top and my shirt hangs over my crotch like this the entire time, my sales record should stand on its own. As for my charming personality…I better hit the bar I saw when I boarded and get a drink before this shitshow starts.

Slipping out into the corridor, I try to orient myself. Aft, bow, forward—I don't know what anything on a boat is called. I realize I'm going the wrong way when the end of the corridor leads to stairs that go to an upper deck. I'm not ready for mingling yet, and the steward *did* say there's more than one bar on this ship, so I ascend.

The ocean greets me, spreading endlessly beyond the nose of the vessel. It's a refreshing change of view and scent from city life. There's no noise from traffic to remind me of being on a schedule. No exhaust from being stuck in gridlock.

Behind me, the familiar sound of ice cubes clinking against glass pulls me from the lapping waves. Spinning around, I find another bar *and* a hot tub. Rich people, man. If I'm ever one of them, I sure as shit am not going to waste a fortune on a floating luxury hotel.

I shield my eyes from the sun and make my way toward the man mixing a drink. It's not a steward, though, that comes into focus. It's that cocky salesman I've run into at a few trade shows over the last year, Rory. I don't even know what region he works in, never see him copied on emails, nor hear about him. How in the hell did he get an invite?

Wait a minute.

Rory.

Rory, who gave me the card to Illusion. This means I'm not the only person on this ship who knows about Illusion. Adjusting myself discreetly, I am more aware now than ever of the cinching sensation around my balls, as if that were possible.

Listen to me. I'm being stupid. It's not like he knows what went down. It's not like he'll be bantering about sex clubs over dinner with McDonnell and the other salespeople.

I have nothing to worry about.

Actually…this could be an opportunity. He might have some answers for me.

"Rory, hey," I greet, sidling up to the opposite side of the bar.

"Hi. Do I know you?"

How can he be a sales rep and not remember names? That's key in our line of work. His grown-out wavy black hairstyle doesn't speak professionalism to me. Or perhaps it's how the sleeves of his white linen button-up are rolled up to his elbows. His shirt collar is spread wide, revealing a thin silver chain and a few curls on his tan chest, while my polo shirt has all the buttons done. He looks like an Italian underwear model who came prepared for beach time, the way he's at home behind the bar, not an anxious salesman wondering why he got invited to a random luxury business cruise.

"Y-eah. Charlie," I remind him. "We chatted at the Seattle convention a few months ago."

"Oh, nice to see you again."

Nodding absently, his attention returns to the garnish tray like olives take precedent over courtesy. Spearing a few, he drops them in his drink and takes a sip, looking satisfied. When he turns and gazes out at the ocean, it's apparent he really doesn't remember me.

How do you hand out a sex club card and not remember who you gave it to? Does he hand out so many that he can't keep track?

In my annoyance, a peculiar thought takes hold. Has he been pleasured by my guy?

My guy. Listen to me. He's not my fucking guy. I'm wasting valuable time before the welcome dinner being a cock suppressed idiot when I could be getting intel.

Leaning against the bar, I clear my throat. "Yeah. You, um… gave me a business card the last time we met."

That gets his attention. Maybe there's hope. Except…now he looks confused.

"I give a lot of those out. My number hasn't changed, if that's what you're asking. Did you need a new one?"

I gape as he reaches into the pocket of his shorts and pulls out his wallet. He can't be serious. My heart sinks when I spot Amor's logo at the corner of a business card he starts to tug out of his billfold. I know my brothers say I'm uptight, but seriously, how do you not remember passing someone a card to a sex club? Maybe it's not as big of a deal to him as it is to me since it was my first time at one.

"No," I digress, trying not to sound agitated as I hold up a hand to stop him. "You gave me…" Fuck. How do I explain this? "A *different* business card. One for…an *attraction* in Seattle."

Frowning, he hums in thought, studying me like my face holds the answer. He's a fucking idiot, clearly, but at least I have his undivided attention now.

Of course, this isn't going to be easy. Why did I think even for a second that it would be? Nothing since the minute I walked into that place has been easy. Sighing, I glance around the deck to make sure no one else has wandered up here before I elaborate. "And *I went*."

Recognition flickers on his face, finally. Brows hiking, he leans on the bar and murmurs conspiratorially, "Ah! And…did you enjoy the amenities?"

What the fuck kind of question is that? Did he think I brought it up just to chit chat like that's the kind of shit I chit chat about with veritable strangers on work trips?

Face burning, I glance toward the stairs again. It's still just the two of us and nothing but the ocean breeze up here. I probably need to admit something if I want to enlist his help.

"Yeah. Plenty of times."

"Hm. Sounds like someone's a little greedy." He chuckles, drawing back and swirling his olive spear around.

Judgement? Really? I'm not the one who carries around the damn club's card in my wallet and hands it out to a complete stranger. Rolling my eyes, I grit my teeth and scan the bottles behind the bar, remembering I came here in search of liquor to take the edge off. That edge has just increased twofold, thanks to Mr. Smug.

"Whatever," I grumble. "I'm single. I work all the damn time."

Following my gaze, he grabs a bottle of scotch from the bar-back setup and raises it in question. If he wants to play bartender, fine by me. It's the least he can do for, in part, getting me into the mess that I'm in. I shrug my shoulder carelessly in approval, and he places a rocks glass in front of me.

"Well, then I'm glad you found something that fits into your schedule. Ice?"

"Yeah. Sure."

Watching him tediously scoop cubes from an ice bucket with a little metal scoop, my line of questioning feels like a snarl of Christmas lights that needs unraveling. I'm not overly social outside of my sales routes, and I can't remember ever talking about sex with anyone. Something about him making me a drink, however, gives off a vibe of camaraderie, bolstering my bravery. I mean, if recommending sex clubs is no big deal to him, I should try to act like it's no big deal to talk about one.

"Have you ever…had a problem…at one of these places?"

"What kind of problem?"

"The kind where…" Jeez. What do I even say? Shifting, my tender nuts beg me to say something. "Like if someone acted inappropriately."

He stops mid-pour. His chestnut gaze flicks to mine with something more threatening in it than I imagined him capable of possessing. Until now, I'd have pegged him for one of those people who are so laid-back it's almost obnoxious. "Did someone hurt you?"

"No," I blurt, taken aback at his level of concern. I don't want this to be a big deal. I want to get the help I need and then have it be a forgettable conversation. "They just…did something I didn't expect."

Brow furrowing, he considers my cryptic admission and finishes his pour. "And you didn't like it?"

I'll give him points for being delicate. I should be grateful he's respecting my apparent desire for privacy by not asking me to elaborate, but his surprising discretion just embarrasses me further. It's embarrassing because my gut instinct suddenly has me wanting to be completely transparent. It's another thing about this entire ordeal that I realized last night—it's left me feeling emotionally vulnerable on a level I've never experienced.

"I…I don't know."

Sliding the rocks glass toward me, he rests his hands on the edge of the bar. Brow creased, he looks rightly stupefied by my contradiction.

Fucking hell. I never imagined talking about my sex life to a complete stranger.

Taking a healthy gulp of my drink, I wait for the burn to make its way down my throat. We're two adults who've both been to a sex club. Get over yourself, Charlie. It's not like the mystery man is here to hear any of this.

"At first it seemed kind of hot," I admit, because…for a few blissful moments in that room, it was. And, if I'm being honest, when I'm not freaking out, it still seems hot for some completely fucked-up reason I can't explain. "But now, no," I affirm. "Not anymore."

"Jeez, I'm sorry I gave you the card then," his reply comes with earnest remorse. "I was just trying to help, I swear." I feel an inch smaller under that odd apology as he takes a drink and then scrubs his hand over his dark stubble. "You know, if you're not up for casual encounters, that might not be the place for you. Maybe get yourself a boyfriend instead."

God. He's missing the point here. Granted, he doesn't know the whole story, but I don't have the patience right now to listen to misguided life advice.

"I don't need or want a boyfriend. I just…need to talk to them about it, but they haven't been back and the doorman won't tell me who it is."

"Privacy is a big part of those places. He's just doing his job."

"I know that, but I have a problem that can't be fixed without knowing who my visitor was."

"You're pregnant?" he asks, smirking.

And there's the fucking Rory I pegged him to be when I noticed that twinkle in his eye the night he gave me that card. What the fuck was I thinking going to a damn place this guy recommended?

"It's not funny." I glower.

"Did you catch something?"

"What?" I'm not sure why I ask for confirmation. I know I heard him correctly. He's looking at me seriously this time, the smar-tass-ness completely gone from his expression, as though he's reigned himself in from my scolding. "No. I get tested, and the club says all their visitors have to show their tests to enter."

"I'm not sure I'm understanding the issue here." He frowns. "What exactly is the problem? Do you have feelings for the person?"

I know I was vague, but damn. That has me snorting. "I don't even know them. How can I have feelings?"

Shrugging, he straightens up and reaches for his glass again. "It's an intimate experience. Of course, feelings can be involved. There's no shame in that."

Wow. That's deep coming from a guy who hands out cards to sex clubs.

"Whatever. No, it's not that."

Sighing, I ease onto a stool and face the ocean view. So much for this brilliant idea. Gazing out at one of the islands in the dis-tance, I accept the fact that I'll just have to hunt down a very expensive and discreet nut specialist to cut through this contrap-tion when I get home. With any luck, I'll get this promotion and not have to bat an eye at the bill.

I feel eyes on me and find Rory squinting at me in thought. "You felt violated in some way and want to talk it out with the man?" he wagers.

Apparently, he didn't know I had given up on his sage advice. I can't believe I'm sitting here talking to him about being possibly '*violated*.' It's kind of hard to consider it a violation when I willingly stuck my cock through a hole, looking for a good time. My *trust*, however, was definitely violated.

"Something like that," I mutter, taking a drink, but find his curious gaze still on me when I finish. The hell with it. I don't need him prodding me about this in front of others on the cruise and accidentally being overheard later. And I don't know a single other person who has been to a sex club.

"He…he *put something* on me." His reply is yet another furrowed brow, so I elaborate, "Something I *can't* get off."

His body flinches backward. "Jesus. Did he brand you or something?"

"What? No. It…"

For a moment, images assault my mind. It makes me realize I had no business walking into that place. Leaning over the bar to whisper, I feel like a complete idiot. There isn't even a bird in sight for miles to overhear me, but leaving Rory to his imagination is clearly a mistake. Branding? Do people actually do that?

"Something *metal…on my cock*."

His eyes widen and his brows hike. "A cage?"

His quick guess has my face burning over my previous ignorance of such things. "Yeah," I mutter, "And he fucking locked it."

The wind whistles around us in the silence that follows. I peek over at him, too curious to see his reaction now that it's had a moment to sink in.

"Wow. He must really like you."

"*Like me?* Who the fuck would do something like that to someone if they like them? I'm fucking miserable. It's been a week."

"Damn. You've got it bad, too."

I blink. Are we even speaking the same language?

"What? What the hell are you talking about?"

Shrugging like I'm missing the obvious, he says matter-of-factly, "You're already longing for your keymaster after only a week."

Keymaster. A rush of blood pulses inside my already engorged flesh at the word. At the same time, common sense and my pre-caged Charlie brain cells see red over the thought of someone claiming ownership over me or a part of my body, and that ownership now being public knowledge.

"I'm not *longing* for *anyone*. I'm *longing* to get this fucking thing off me and get my dick back."

"You're sure?" Why he looks so fucking quizzical asking mo that is astounding.

"Yes, I'm sure! What kind of question is that?"

"Well, you went there for an experience, right? Maybe you should make sure you consider that so you don't have any regrets about removing it preemptively, in case it's just a matter of you not being comfortable admitting the thrill of the chase to yourself."

Oh, for fuck's sake with this guy.

"'*Thrill of the chase*?' Are you out of your fucking mind? I've been wearing this thing all fucking week at work, making sure no one is in the bathroom each time I have to take a piss, wondering if it's going to be stuck on me the rest of my life. What thrill is there in that?"

His eyes seem to soften, and his lower lip pouts sympathetically as he leans on the bar. "I doubt that's what your man intended," he soothes, startling me when his hand rests gently over the top of my wrist. "Giving someone a cage is a huge compliment. It means they're so taken with you they can't bear the thought of sharing you with yourself or anyone else, and that the idea of you being hard and craving only them for relief is…well, if you ask me, there's nothing more erotically intimate than that type of connection. Can you imagine? *Needing someone* on that level? The passion would be endless."

My throat is completely parched, making me think I wouldn't be able to respond even if I could find words as I stare at the peculiar daze that seems to have come over Rory's eyes. The fantasy he described pulled not only himself onto a higher plane, but me as well. My chest is heavy. My lungs are burning under my rampant heartbeat at the thought of what he described. Someone being so taken with me they can't stand the thought of me getting pleasure from anyone but them. It's nothing I ever imagined turning me on.

It's not.

It isn't. It's ridiculous.

It's this fucking cage, fucking with my blood supply and my brain. What he described is a fairytale and the asshole behind the panel was just a sick bastard playing a cruel joke because that's the way life works. Tugging my hand away nonchalantly, I pick up my drink and wet my lips.

"Well, I don't need *him*. I just need my dick back so I can get on with my life. Now, can you help me or not? Do you know anyone at the club you could maybe talk to…discreetly?"

Blowing out a breath, he retreats from my personal bubble and tucks his hands in his back pockets. "Rules are rules, I'm afraid. I'm sorry. Have you tried picking the lock?"

"Of fucking course I have."

"Are you hard right now?"

I choke on my scotch and come up sputtering. "What?"

That gets me a peculiar look. He motions with his head toward the stairwell to the deck below us. "I've got some lube in my room. You can get them off sometimes, carefully, without the key, but it won't be easy if you're hard."

Oh. That's why he wanted to know. Prize idiot award to Charlie North. *Am I* uptight?

"No. I'm not fucking hard," I say dryly, trying to sound frustrated and less like an embarrassed virgin. "Why would I be?"

For some reason, he snorts. What the heck is that smirk for? Slapping me on the shoulder, he nods toward the stairwell. "Easy, tough guy. Come on, then. We've got an hour before dinner. Let's see if we can set you free."

He starts strolling toward the stairs, drink in hand. He can't be serious.

"What? *Right now?* With *you?*"

"Well, it doesn't sound like you've had much luck on your own." Glancing back, he bats his eyelashes. "I'll be gentle. I promise."

I sit like dead weight, contemplating how good or bad an idea it is to enlist the help of a guy who gave me a card to a sex club in removing a cage. I can honestly see both the pros and the cons. The thought of showing my debacle to anyone, however, is as enticing as going at the cable again with wire snippers.

"Unless," he adds thoughtfully, "you'd prefer to wait for your master?"

My feet hit the deck a second later. This cocky ass prick.

"Where's your fucking room?"

CHAPTER 7

After following Rory's tediously lazy stroll to his cabin, it hits me I've never been exposed to anyone in the daylight before, when he closes the door. The sheer number of windows in his room seems excessive. Granted, they're not floor-to-ceiling, but there's enough sun pooling in that it doesn't leave many shadows, even with the lights off.

It probably doesn't help that the focal point of the room is the massive bed in the center. It makes it feel like we're about to do something intimate, even though there's nothing sexual about this. I'm not even attracted to him. There's no denying he's handsome, but he's not my type—if I were to even have one. He's far too smug with his calm, confident persona. Something about it… irks me for some reason. I don't care that he didn't bat an eye at my predicament or that he's been discreet about it thus far. He's basically the last person I would choose to help me out, but my stupid pride and misery triumphed over my common sense.

"You certainly scored a nice cabin," I say to break the awkward silence as he makes his way to the dresser and desk below a big screen at the end of the bed and sets his drink down.

"Did you get a double and not like your roommate?"

"No." I shrug, like I even knew getting saddled with a roommate was a possibility. "Your cabin is just clearly bigger."

How in the hell he scored a larger room than me, I'd like to know. Was it by chance, or does it have something to do with being in the running for the promotion? I will be pissed if he gets the job over me.

"Count yourself lucky. The cabins on this deck are kings. The lower deck cabins are all doubles," he says, patting me on the shoulder as he walks by. "Make yourself comfortable. I'll go get what we need."

The fact he knows one more bit of information that I don't grates on my nerves. If that welcoming gesture and suggestion were meant to put me at ease, they didn't work. I watch him disappear into his bathroom, leaving me alone in his temporary dwelling.

Exhaling, I pace past the bed, taking in the rest of the room. It's tidy. Not a sight of luggage or clothing strewn anywhere. He's either neat and already unpacked or stowed his suitcase in a cabinet when he arrived. The only personal items I find are three books and a pair of reading glasses on the nightstand. They conflict with the piecemeal image I have of him. A mischievous jokester who fawns over the garnish tray behind a bar and hands out sex-club cards doesn't seem like someone who spends his evenings quietly reading in bed.

Not that I give a damn what makes him tick. I just can't believe I let him dare me into following him here because he dropped the word, keymaster. Huffing, I sit down on the end of the bed, lest I look like I'm spying on his personal space when he returns. My ass no sooner touches the mattress than he breezes through the bathroom doorway with a black toiletries bag and washcloth tucked under his arm.

"Got it," he calls, walking over to an ottoman that's stowed underneath the desk. Sliding it out, he gives it a push with his foot toward me and straddles it. "Okay, let's see what we're working with here."

He could lose the chipper air. It's not like we're buddies. I can't believe he's cool with this. The more I can't believe it, the more I hate how uptight that must make me seem. Rolling my eyes, I rise and clench my teeth. Reaching for my zipper, I focus on my fingers and not on the fact I'm about to show my caged dick to another man who's just mere inches away from it. I don't know why I'm so uncomfortable if he doesn't seem to give a shit. Maybe it's because I've never been semi-naked in front of someone if it wasn't for sex. Maybe it's because I can smell his scent, and it's not a terrible scent. Maybe it's because I know he's into guys, too.

None of that matters, though, I decide. I'm uncomfortable because someone slapped a cage on my cock and this feels like a bizarre doctor's appointment. Still, it will be better than an actual doctor's appointment. Hooking my thumbs into the waistband of my boxer briefs and shorts, I hold my breath and shove them down over my ass. It lowers them to my upper thigh, just enough that I'll be able to show him the mess that I'm in. My shirt is still hanging down, covering me up, but I can feel the air on my exposed skin. The lines at the corners of Rory's dark eyes show he's poised, patiently awaiting the big reveal.

God help me.

Letting out a breath, I pinch my eyes shut, grab the hem of my shirt, and lift it. My heartbeat flutters erratically. The combination of feeling naked and exposed with my eyes closed is like being back in that room. Except, this time it's not pleasure that awaits me. It's judgment. I wait for laughter, a snort, something that will make me further regret following this eccentric man into his cabin.

A low whistle splits the silence.

"That's a nice model. Top of the line."

It's the last thing I expected to hear, forcing a disbelieving puff of laughter from my throat. "Thanks. I get that all the time."

"I bet you do."

Before I can process how that oddly sounded like flirting, he rests his bag on his lap and tugs my shorts lower, making them fall from my grasp. Instinct has me wanting to bend to catch them as they slide down my legs, but standing between Rory and the bed makes that difficult.

When they reach my ankles, he steps on them with one of his flip-flops. Reaching down, he wraps a hand around my calf like he wants me to lift my leg and step out of them.

"Uh, I don't think that's necessary," I complain, letting my shirt fall and doing my best to stay rooted to the carpeting.

Clicking his tongue, he chides, "I need room to work. Sit down, will you?"

Fucking hell. Why can't I be as blasé about this as him? It's not like I agreed to come in here just for a peep show. Gathering my patience, whatever the fuck is left of it, I grudgingly plop my ass down on the bed, holding my shirt down over my junk.

Should I have asked for a towel? Is it rude to sit bare-assed on someone else's bed?

I feel my leg lifted, only realizing too late that sitting took my weight off my feet. Every fiber in me wants to be a prude and protest that him freeing my foot from my shorts and underwear was not needed, but I've already made a big enough crybaby of myself today. I'm aware I can't sit here with my knees locked together. To look at his face, you'd think this was as mundane a task as filling out a travel reimbursement voucher, telling me I'm the only one freaking out. I need to get a grip.

I try not to go rigid when he leans into my space, wondering what the hell he's doing. His skin is warm against mine, where his leg hair brushes against my shins. I covertly let out my breath when I see that he's just setting his bag down on the bed next to me. He sure has no problem with personal space. His hair is nearly brushing my cheek. It's so thick and healthy looking, not a strand of gray. I'm curious how old he is, but not enough to ask. There's something in the way a man's muscle tone sits on him, though—the way he ages into his physique, built but tawny—that makes me think he's a few years older than me. Mentally, I begrudgingly award him more points for aging well.

His cotton shirt feels like a bed sheet rubbing against my bare knee as he unzips and rifles through his bag while I try to focus on a spot on the wall. I feel something fall onto the comforter next to me but refuse to look when looking would put our faces closer together than necessary. Something grazes the side of my ass cheek, sending a shiver up my spine. It was only for a split second, and I'm sure it wasn't intentional, but I'm fairly certain it was the back of his fingers. I'm trying not to squirm, but everything in me wants to come up with some polite way to decline this ludicrous offer of assisting me. What the fuck can he do that I haven't already tried?

Sitting back, he pops the lid on a sizable bottle of lube. This cruise is only three nights. Who would need that much lube for a three-night work cruise? Curiosity has me glancing down at his toiletry bag now that he's not digging in it. My throat goes dry as though I'm viewing Pandora's box.

A thick black dildo takes up the length of the bag. It's veiny and ribbed close to the tip. But that's not even the showstopper. It's the entirety of the bag's contents. There are two different sizes of anal plugs and a spiky silicone cock ring. What in the hell was he planning to get up to on this trip? There's only one overnight stop scheduled, and I'm pretty sure all the other salesmen are straight.

"Whenever you're ready." His low voice snaps my attention back to the matter at hand.

I'm clutching the hem of my shirt down over my cock again like a virgin, completely at odds with my bare ass on his bed. I came here of my own accord, and now it's go time. Right.

At least looking at my contraption will keep his gaze off the shade of red that's probably coloring my face. Lifting the fabric, I fold it in on itself to stay in place against my stomach as I watch him squeeze a bead of lube onto his index finger.

His bare foot slides along the inside of my ankle, making me tense when his knee follows. It presses against mine, urging it outward. My eyes dart to his with the new knowledge of what a can must feel like when it's being pried open.

"Easy," he soothes. "You need to spread your legs more so I can see what I'm doing."

"I think you've seen more than most already," I huff, shifting on the bed but widening my legs a fraction.

He lets out a breathless laugh, scooching forward. It brings his knee higher up the inside of my thigh. I feel slick skin against skin on the sensitive flesh around my sac where the cable is pressing—his fingertip…covered in lube. The air in my lungs forms a painful bubble. He's…basting the tender skin there. His touch, gentle…soothing, even.

"Not like one of those rooms, is it?" he remarks softly. The small bit of understanding is enough to relax my rigid spine a fraction, and then he makes a sympathetic noise. "You're getting raw here. Have you been putting lube around the ring?"

"No," I grump, refusing to sound like everyone should know what to do with these things.

I make the mistake of glancing down, curious if my sore flesh became hideous overnight. The sight of him crooking his slathered finger and the sensation of relief it's bringing me has my blood going warm. It's a surreal sensation of being cared for when I least expected it. And then my gaze meets his, sending a wash of flames up my face. It makes this all too much of a reality for my liking, so I quickly look away, staring toward his cabin windows.

"I wouldn't have pegged you for the shy type."

"Shy's got nothing to do with it. What's your plan here, anyway?"

I hear the squelch of the lube bottle, and then his index finger returns along with his middle one, following the cable to the underside of my balls. That puts him dangerously close to my taint. My heartbeat is pounding in my ears. If I hold my breath any longer, I might pass out.

"These things can come off without unlocking them," he says lazily. "You just have to work your cock backward through the ring, and then it's more manageable to work your sac out, but I don't know if that's going to work right now."

No shit. What a fucking genius.

"I can't work my cock backward. I'll fucking break it."

"Yeah, you will with how hard you are right now," he agrees, but it's not the hint of mirth in his voice that has me looking back at him. My balls feel extra snug suddenly, as if that were possible, and…warm. Glancing down, I suck in a gasp. His palm is cupping my protruding, caged sac. "And I hate to break it to you, but *these*," he adds, giving them a gentle rub that has me biting back a whimper, "are so fucking full, there's no way we're going to be able to slip them through the ring like this. It's too tight. You need to come if you want any chance of getting out of this thing."

I blink at him, trying to absorb his words. I know I heard him, but that warm palm cupping my balls has short-circuited something in my brain, robbing me of my ability to speak. It's my weakness—how pleasure feels immeasurably better when the touch comes from someone other than myself. Something about this damn cage, though, is making me hyper responsive to that barest of contact, like my cock is beholden to someone who would set it free. To a…keymaster.

I don't realize I'm still staring at him until he remarks curiously, "For someone who wants this off so badly, you don't seem to be hating it." Eyes narrowing in thought, he mumbles almost like he's talking to himself, "Unless…"

"Unless what?" I let out in a breathy rush.

"Unless…you like showing it off to me."

It's the first time he hasn't smirked or had that wicked glint in his eyes. He looks perfectly serious. And maybe it's all the damn blood rushed to my groin, starving my brain of oxygen, but a charge of static electricity flutters down my legs over how it almost looks like he's hopeful my answer will be an affirmative.

What the fuck is that about?

This is Rory. Rory, who I barely know and works for the same fucking company that I do. Rory, who's on a work cruise with me, holding my fucking balls in his hand in a cabin on a cruise ship owned by the damn CEO of the company. Rory, who invited me in here to help me out of this thing, not to make a pass at me. Like I could fucking do anything in this damn cage right now, anyway, even if I did want to. What kind of cruel human being is he?

"Yeah. That's exactly what I'm doing!" I snap, slapping his hand away. "Dropping trou in front of a stranger so I can hear smug jokes while he fondles my balls under false pretenses." Leaning to the side, I reach down for my shorts. "You said you could help, jackass. Thanks for nothing."

"Whoa. Hey, hey. I didn't mean any offense," he soothes, placing his hands on my shoulders and putting himself in my field of vision. "I'm sorry. Come on. I'm only human." He shrugs. "You have to admit it's kind of hot. Certainly, the highlight of this trip so far for me." He flashes an impish grin at me.

I sit back but still try to work my shorts up my leg with my foot to let him know where he can stick his apology. Grimacing, he pats the top of my knee and holds up an index finger.

"Just a minute. There's one other thing we can try. I've got some tweezers. Maybe I can pick the lock."

Yanking my shirt over my dick again, I huff, but stay seated for the mere fact that walking would be too painful right now. I don't know how to take him or his backhanded compliments. *He's only human?* What the hell was that supposed to mean? And how can this be hot to him if I can't use my dick?

"Yeah. Good luck," I grumble. "I've already tried that." My warning doesn't seem to deter him as he rifles through his bag of toys. "What's with all the shit in your bag? Do you always pack like that for work trips?"

Brandishing a pair of tweezers, he smiles like it's a fucking key to my problems. "I like to be prepared. Life is short. I'm not one to pass up a good time."

He has no idea. "Yeah, well, word to the wise. Be careful what you wish for." I gesture to my junk and casually pull my shirt up again, although not as high as last time.

My dick jostles, telling me he's holding the cage. I pinch my eyes shut, trying to snuff out the sensations.

His soft hum helps to distract me. "I had one of these years ago. I was skeptical about it at first, too."

"*At first?* How long did you have it?"

"Mm, about a year."

"A *year?* You wore one of these for a year? How the fuck did you manage that?"

The side of his finger grazes the tender flesh of my cock through the rings of the cage as he tilts it to the side. I can feel his hair brushing against the top of my thigh, feel his warm breath on my cock, making it tingle. I hope by some miracle he can get it off. Better I embarrass myself by being turned on in front of another gay man than in front of a potentially straight doctor I'd have to pay when I get home. I just hope Rory doesn't think I'm hard because of him. It's not because of him. It's this fucking cage.

"It was fine." He laughs. "Great, actually. You get used to it. Like I said, it heightens the anticipation of when you do see the person. I'd be sitting in class, knowing that every time the professor looked at me, he was the only one who could let me out…it made it this erotic secret between the two of us."

"Your fucking professor caged you?"

"Yeah. Robert. Good old Rob." He lets out a happy-sounding sigh. "I still think about those days sometimes. Best year of my life."

I can't even imagine having had the courage to approach one of my professors or accepting their flirting if they had been the first to initiate when I was in college, let alone being open to being caged by someone in my early twenties. Nothing about Rory's reaction makes me doubt he enjoyed his experience. My situation, however, is totally different. If he meant to cheer me up, he didn't. All I feel is jealousy. *Good old Rob* clearly gave a damn about him.

"Yeah, well, at least that was consensual, not some stranger who slapped one on you and then disappeared without a backward glance."

"Oh, I'm sure he'll come back. Nobody would do this to be cruel."

"I went back at our usual time, and he wasn't there."

He makes that obnoxious, thoughtful humming noise he does. "I'm sure he had a good reason. If he's seen this cock and caged it, he's definitely got plans for it."

If he's seen *this cock?* What's that supposed to mean? Is he… flirting with me again?

"Well, the good news and the bad news is that this is a custom cage," he continues. "It was made with love. Two locking mechanisms. It's a masterpiece, really."

My cock jostles again as he demonstrates what I already know, pointing out how I need the numeric code to be set for the key to engage a second locking mechanism on the bottom. Now that I think about it, he probably fucking knew that even before he got out his damn tweezers. I suddenly can't take Rory's comfortable touch, his smooth voice, or being talked about like sexual property any longer.

Nudging his hand away, I rise. "You know what? I've got this," I inform him, stepping to the side out from between him and the end of the bed so I can grab my shorts. "Thanks for the help, but I'm sure you've got better things to do."

"Not really, but suit yourself." His overly pleased expression lets me know what a fool I just made of myself before I stomp out of the cabin, no freer than when I entered. I don't even get the luxury of blowing off steam by taking a long walk down the corridor because, wouldn't you know my luck—mine is right fucking next to his.

CHAPTER 8

I contemplated having some alone time with my electric razor prior to dinner to clear my head but decided not to chance ending up a crying mess again. That's not how I plan on meeting McDonnell and facing the other sales reps tonight. So, here I am, heading down the corridor toward the dining lounge, just as fired up as when I arrived, if not more so.

Fucking Rory and his stupid, low-key flirting. I will not give him the satisfaction of accidentally overhearing me try to get myself off. An entire ship and he has to be my freaking neighbor. Whatever. Only three nights. At least I didn't have to room with someone like he mentioned. I couldn't imagine getting caught undressing in front of Niel or any of the other salesmen that I know.

Exhaling, I make my way toward the sounds of music and the familiar laughter of people I know, co-workers I've seen on web meetings and at conventions countless times. I have what it takes to oversee the company's marketing team, don't I?

I mean, I know I got this invite, but I can do it. I can. I'm not just fluffing my feathers. I kind of wish my boss hadn't let me in on the secret though. If I didn't know about the opening, then I wouldn't have any cause to be disappointed if I didn't get it.

Right. Maybe it's the hype that's been getting to me and not my nuts after all.

That line of thinking puts me at ease so much that I find myself smiling when Carmen and Niel wave me over to where they're sitting at the bar. I order a drink and take in the long dining table in the middle of the room. It's complete with fancy table settings, candles, and folded linen napkins. The hors d'oeuvres that Carmen and Niel are fawning over at the bar show that no expense has been spared for us on this trip.

"Can you believe all this?" Carmen remarks, flipping her long braids over the shoulder strap of her cocktail dress. "I take back anything bad I've ever said about this company."

"I'm telling you," Niel pipes in, spearing a bacon-wrapped water chestnut, "look around. There are only twelve of us sales reps from all the regions. That means they're fattening us up for the kill. I bet they're going to downsize and double our workload, and this is the last hurrah before our nose is to the grindstone, and our territories triple in size."

Swatting his arm with the back of her hand, Carmen gives him a harsh whisper, "Stop it. Maybe we just got called here for incentive rewards. Either way, I'm going to enjoy myself, damn it."

"Fine, but don't say I didn't warn you," Niel lets out with a sigh, shaking his head.

"Nuh uh. You're not going to ruin this for me." She holds up a finger, turning her back to him. "What do you think, Charlie? Don't tell me you share Mr. Doom and Gloom's theory."

I don't know if it would be kind to let her in on my knowledge, but I'm too distracted by the sight across the room at the moment to do so. A salesman from the East Coast steps away from a leather sectional that wraps around the corner of the room, revealing Rory. I didn't know the man could clean up so well.

At the few conventions I've seen him at, he was either in a sweater or a casual blazer. Tonight, he's opted for a black suit jacket and a crisp white dress shirt, un-fucking-buttoned, of course, and no tie. Why does he still look better than I do? Even his unruly hair looks like he gave it some attention and gelled it back, making him more presentable for a formal setting. Who the fuck is he trying to impress?

His head turns away from whomever he's listening to, and his gaze meets mine, but his smile doesn't falter. All I can see on his face is my dirty little secret, his slick fingers on my balls, the playful glint in his eyes from earlier, and that fancy-ass suit he clearly wore to steal my fucking promotion.

Fucking hell. Why did I ever trust him? He'll dime me out in a heartbeat. I just know it.

There's something…intimidating about him, which is bonkers. Nothing about the guy should be intimidating. When his mouth isn't ticked up at the corner, he's quiet in thought with this deep, far-off look in his eyes like he knows secrets of the world that no one else does. It's…unsettling. I don't even know how he got invited on this cruise. I'd love to find out his sales record. Guaranteed, I freaking smoked his, but that delighted look in his eyes right now tells me that the first chance he gets McDonnell alone, he'll spill the beans about why I'm not a good candidate for the job.

"Charlie…"

"What?" Snapping my attention back to Carmen, I find her flashing me a peculiar look.

"Are you all right?"

"Yeah. Fine. I'm fine. What were you saying?"

"We were just wondering what your take on this all-expenses-paid cruise was? Does McDonnell have evil plans for all of us, or is he really the best CEO to have ever CEO'd?"

A steward, dressed in a formal uniform for the evening, calls for our attention near the doorway. He makes the announcement that dinner is ready to be served and for us to take our seats.

"I doubt it's anything malicious," I inform Carmen, taking her hand to help her from her stool as she gathers her drink. The least I can do is *not* burst her bubble.

As we step toward the dining table, I notice there are place cards in front of each of the chairs. Assigned seating. What the hell does that mean? Is there a pecking order?

I feel an elbow in my ribs, and Carmen whispers in my ear as she nudges me toward the head of the table. "Tell me if you find anything out."

I spot my name at a seat right next to the end of the table. Right next to the head of the table, to be exact. That has to be a good sign, right? Maybe my boss knew what he was talking about after all.

Taking my seat carefully, I try not to wince at the awkward sensation against my nether region. It is so incredibly bizarre to be sitting in a room full of my work counterparts, wearing a cock cage under the table, unbeknownst to them. Well, all of them except one. Where the fuck is Rory?

Glancing down the table, I find every single chair is occupied. Did he skip out or something? He's honestly so eccentric, it doesn't surprise me that—

"Good evening, everyone."

The smooth, deep voice that I remember from earlier comes from above me to my right. I follow the crisp dress shirt and black suit jacket up to find Rory's intelligent eyes twinkling in the candlelit room, a hush going over the table. What the fuck is he doing?

"I think I've gotten the chance to meet most of you, but for those I haven't, I'm Riordan McDonnell, CEO of Amor. On behalf of myself and the company, I'd like to welcome you to this appreciation cruise for all your hard work this past fiscal year."

His mouth keeps moving. Words keep coming out. Professional words, free of sarcasm or innuendo, but I stop hearing them after that. All I hear is *CEO of Amor. CEO* as in…CEO of the fucking company that I work for. *CEO,* as in the guy who will be picking who gets the promotion. McDonnell. *Rory McDonnell…*

Rory is Riordan McDonnell?

Why didn't I take one of his fucking business cards when I had the chance?

No. What did I do instead? Showed him my dick and asked zero questions later. *Holyfuckingshit!* I never cared that our company doesn't have pictures of our sales reps or board members on its website until this moment.

"Charlie?"

"Huh?"

He's seated now. When the hell did he stop talking and sit down?

The steward is holding a tray of salads. Rory's curious gaze flicks from mine to the steward like an instruction. I mumble something unintelligible and sit back to allow the man to place a bowl in front of me, and then he moves on. When he rounds the table to the salesman across from me, I finally find the nerve to speak again.

"*Riordan?*" I mutter accusingly under my breath, realizing my theory about him looking like an Italian model has been blown entirely out of the water by his Irish-sounding name.

There's that annoying hum. "Yes. But…my friends call me Rory."

Friends. Am *I* supposed to be his fucking friend? I can't be his friend. I work for him.

You know what else I can't be? The guy who shows him a fucking cock cage!

Fortunately, everyone sitting around us is eager to speak to the elusive CEO we've never set eyes on before. That affords me the luxury of silently reliving every embarrassing interaction I had with the man. Maybe the yacht will sail close enough to shore so I can grab a life preserver and jump overboard.

When dinner is cleared, I still haven't looked at him once, but there's no way to salvage this. Even if he doesn't give a damn if his employees wear cock cages, how in the hell could I ever work directly under him knowing what he knows and has seen what he's seen?

I couldn't. I just couldn't. I can barely sit next to him as it is. My skin is on fire. And the most bizarre thing is that…I feel like I've somehow betrayed that asshole from the club who put the cage on me by showing it to Rory. I swear, for once in my life, I think I'm honestly considering the idea of getting a boyfriend, just as Rory suggested. I doubt, however, a boyfriend could supply that level of desire a cage is supposed to represent, the way Rory described in his cabin earlier today.

Listen to me. Thinking of getting a boyfriend. I'm just sick of being in hell and sick of the wrong people knowing about it.

When the steward starts clearing the table for dessert, I have every intention of hopping up out of my seat to excuse myself. Gerald, the salesman seated across from me, however, says the most idiotic thing I've heard.

"Divine has nothing on Amor. Our sales beat theirs five to one," he boasts in response to Rory's mention of one of the top chocolate competitors.

"Actually, they outsell us three to one," I correct, unable to help myself. When it comes to statistics, I can't keep silent.

Scoffing, Gerald's cheeks go pink as he glances from Rory to me. "Um, no, *actually*. Hardly any of my suppliers carry them in my region."

"You're what—in the north? Most of your suppliers deliver from Canada, right?"

At that, he nods suspiciously. I can feel Rory's eyes on me, but I ignore the weight of how his gaze makes me feel. I still have a job at the moment. I might as well pretend like I do, even if it's just for one more evening.

"Divine is a European-based company. You're getting their duties from Canada on your shipments, which your suppliers might not want to pay. And I meant they outsell us three to one across the board, not just in your region. You have to look at our competitors' sales as a whole, not just from the territory you work in." While I'm aware how flawless my argument was, it looks like I'm trying too hard to dig my way out of cock-cage hell, so I sit back and shrug like it's not that important of a topic, finishing with, "So they *do*… have something on us."

Snickering an ugly noise, Gerald tries to sound like he's making a joke. "Jeez, who do you work for? Them or us?"

I refuse to be baited into a squabble in front of the man who massaged my cage cable with lube mere hours ago. Those chestnut eyes of his flick to mine and hold my gaze with something that almost looks like appreciation.

Was it all a game to him, I wonder? Did he know he wouldn't be able to get the cage off me? Did he know I had no clue who he was? Does he seriously not care and still want the best man for the job?

A plate is thrust between us. There's a delectable-looking little mound of chocolate cake on it with some type of fancy, hardened chocolate web covering it. Even the plate circumference is adorned with a swirled design of chocolate syrup, more fitting nods to our company's products.

"What is that?" Gerald asks.

"Hazelnut caged mud pie," the steward informs him regally.

My gaze flits to Rory's over the sinful dessert because of-fucking-course it does. *Caged?* Did he just say '*caged*?' I'm met with Riordan McDonnell's poker face, which sears me to the depths of my flesh.

Smiling at the steward, he reaches for the plate. "That sounds absolutely delicious, Ben. I'll take that."

"And you, sir?"

I hop up faster than I intend to, bashing my knee against the table as I do. "Um…no. No, thank you. I'm good."

There is no way I'm sitting here watching Rory break through a chocolate cage with his fork and then shove it in his mouth. I don't know if I expect something, some type of explanation, but when I get back to my cabin, I sit there for what feels like hours, waiting. After a cold shower and the television on low, I lie awake in bed, listening to the sounds of the ship. Finally, I hear footsteps by the door to my cabin. They slow. I think they may even stop outside because my pulse quickens, but then they move on.

It's better this way, I tell myself in the silence that follows. I don't need some awkward apology over my embarrassment from earlier. Clearly, Rory McDonnell is a man of the world, and I am not. Some people know the ins and outs of sex clubs and cock cages and some don't. Some people don't bat an eye at them, while others do. No matter what happened, he can't say it's had any effect on my work performance. What I do in my personal life should be no concern of his. He gave me that fucking card, after all. Part of me, however, still wants this freaking promotion. I know this company and don't want to start over somewhere else. I also don't want to stay and keep running the same sales routes over and over for the next ten years. If Rory can stand to work directly over a guy with a kink, then why shouldn't I be able to stand working directly under a guy who's…who's eccentric in his own right? It's not like I'd even have to see him much.

Sighing, I click the TV off and roll onto my side, closing my eyes. Tomorrow is a new day. I'll just lie low for the day trip they have planned to the island and keep to myself. If he wants to meet with me, I'll keep it all business this time. Now that I know who he is, I won't be shooting the shit and divulging my soul to him again.

CHAPTER 9

Missing the continental breakfast for sleeping in was well worth it. I was able to score a cup of coffee and not have to see a single soul other than the yacht staff. I even took my time exploring the ship after I was assured that '*Mr. McDonnell went ashore with the rest of his guests after breakfast.*'

Being that I've never been to Hawaii before, though, I head off the ship and onto the boardwalk, where I hail a cab. The colorful takes me around the island, giving me a pocket tour which I enjoy as much as one who's hard up in a cock cage can. With the windows down and the island air flowing in, though, I have to say it does something to appease my soul. I can kind of see how people like Rory might think throwing money at a yacht is a worthy expense.

Ha! People like Rory. As if there are others.

What am I saying? There's a whole club back home full of people like Rory. Am I…one of them? I went there too. More than once. *Greedy*, he called me. Was I greedy?

Maybe I was. Look where it got me.

"We can head back now," I inform the driver, a sudden sadness making my chest tighten.

I just…wanted to feel good. I wanted to feel good the only way I knew how. Was that so much to ask? That guy didn't have to leave me high and dry.

Rory said no one would do this to be cruel. That the man had plans for me if he put my cock in a cage. Does that mean he came back? What if he came back when I wasn't there? Fuck. Maybe I missed my chance by being on this stupid cruise and letting Rory lube up my sore balls for nothing. I wish he'd never told me that story about him and his stupid professor. It's a fantasy. I'm sure bonds like that only happen once in a blue moon and certainly only with people of the right mindset. Which I'm not. Look how miserable I've been. It's why I can't understand why Rory's suggestion of finding a boyfriend keeps flitting through my mind. I'm probably just depressed. Depressed at not being able to use my dick.

I have the driver drop me off at a hotel near the dock, where I grab lunch on the patio to eat my feelings. I know we have until evening before roll call on the ship, but my sightseeing ambitions are over for the day, short of trying to relax some of the tension from my body. Heading to reception, I inquire about their spa, only to learn that their masseuses are booked up for the day. Why did I even check? I should just assume by now that there's a black cloud following me overhead.

Heading back toward the dock, I console myself. I have an entire superyacht all to my lonesome for the evening, fully equipped with not one but two hot tubs. That will have to do.

Back in my cabin, I slip into my trunks and grab a towel from the bathroom. It shouldn't take me as much time as it does to decide on which hot tub to head toward—the one on the lower deck or the one up on the flydeck, which I've learned it's called. While the one on the flydeck reminds me of where I first ran into Rory on the yacht, the one on the lower deck is in a prime spot where I'll be seen by anyone who happens to return to the ship early, so up I go.

As I ascend the stairs to the flydeck, though, I hear Carmen's infectious laughter. It's par for the course that I can't find any damn privacy.

At least, it's only her, but still. As long as I can slip in without her noticing anything clinging to my metal-shaped bulge downtown, I should be fine. Ascending the last stair, I stop in my tracks, fully convinced now about that black cloud. It's Carmen and…Rory.

Fuck.

"Hey! Where have you been all day? You missed everything!" Carmen scolds me.

"I…took a tour of the island," I blurt, holding my hands in front of my waist so my towel hangs over my groin.

"What? By yourself? You should have told me. I would have gone with you."

"It was fine. I caught up on some sleep and then just did some sightseeing." I wave a hand dismissively and turn to head back down the stairs, but her voice cuts me off.

"Where are you going? Aren't you getting in?"

"No. I don't want to interrupt."

"You're not interrupting anything, I can assure you," Rory chuckles along with her, telling me I've clearly missed some inside joke.

I turn back around, prepared to say that there's not enough room, but that would be a lie. It's the biggest fucking hot tub I've ever seen. *And* I have my shorts on and am holding a towel. If I leave, I'll look like I'm avoiding Rory.

Son of a bitch.

Kicking my flip-flops off, I curse my fortune and make my way to the side of the tub farthest from Rory. Turning to the side, I try to act casual, bending over and placing my towel down for easy access when it comes time to get out. It's just an excuse to hide my girded loins from the two of them. Stepping backward over the edge of the tub, I dip one foot in the water, performing the world's most awkward descent into a hot tub. Fuck if I'm turning around to face either of them with wet trunks on, though, until my waist is below the surface. Carmen can think I have the grace of a drunk gazelle for all I care.

"Nice, isn't it?" she sighs, leaning her head back on the edge of the tub.

It would be nicer if my cage hadn't just made a soft thunk noise as it tapped the seat of the hot tub. It would also be nicer if I were alone and not four feet away from a wet, shirtless CEO who's seen my cock in a cage and palmed my nuts. But that's just me.

"Yeah. It's great."

"Honestly, Charlie, are you having a good time at all?" she asks, tilting her head with a tone of motherly concern shining through her cheery expression.

"I said it was great." I let out on a puff of forced laughter, turning a palm up as I sling my elbow over the side of the tub. "But just out of curiosity, how many margaritas have you had?"

"Two. One for each of my children." Reaching out, she picks up her salt-rimmed glass off the ledge and takes a sip. "This one is for my husband."

"That could account for why I don't appear to be as chipper as you, but trust me, I'm overjoyed on the inside." Lies. All fucking lies, but I'm a salesman, after all.

Chuckling, she sets her drink back down. "Oh! I know what'll cheer you up. You can join our game."

"Game?" I glance around, although I don't know what I expect to find up here on the flydeck. A chess set, maybe?

"Yeah, we're playing Truth or Truth."

Oh, brother. Only three margaritas?

"Do you mean Truth or Dare?"

"No. *Truth or Truth*," she affirms. "We decided that Truth or Dare might require getting out, so we altered the game for the time being."

I glance at Rory, whose eyes are closed, his head leaning back with the hint of a smile on his face. Truth or Truth would have been a nice game when I first ran into him up here yesterday.

"I think I'll pass, but thanks."

"Oh, come on!" Carmen moans. "I already know plenty about you, and Rory's not judgmental, so you've got nothing to worry about."

"It's all right, Carmen," Rory pipes in. "Some people just like their privacy."

Is he…sticking up for me? And I love how we're all on a first-name basis now. Does that mean she showed him *her* chastity cage? This is so fucking awkward.

I have to say, however, that the soothing sensation of the water on my tense muscles and my heavy-laden cock are balancing out some of my discomfort. My dick almost feels buoyant, submerged deep in the tub. It's a strange sensation after walking around with the cage weighing me down for the past week. It makes it feel like something is missing.

"I think it's your turn in the hot seat anyway," Rory reminds her.

"I have two teenagers. Nothing scares me," she boasts. "Ask away."

"Charlie? Do you want to take this one?" Rory asks, pulling himself up out of the tub. "I need a refill."

I had tried not to notice what was beneath the surface on his side of the tub, but underwater lights left little to the imagination. His tall frame rises as he turns to step out onto the flydeck in a snug-fitting black Speedo. Rivulets of water trickle down his legs, the dark hair plastered to the definition in his muscles. I wish I possessed that part of his demeanor—neither overconfident nor insecure. Averting my gaze from his obscenely fit profile, I focus on Carmen. The last thing I need is Rory McDonnell thinking I'm checking him out.

"Give me your best shot," Carmen challenges, grinning like a tipsy Cheshire Cat.

At least one of us is having a good time. Good for her. I find myself smirking and shaking my head at my friend.

Watching her adjust one of her large hoop earrings, it occurs to me that she's a bit more glammed up in the jewelry department than the times I see her at conventions. There's a tennis bracelet on her wrist with tiny diamonds and a silver chain with a small diamond pendant resting between her clavicles. I'm not looking for state secrets since I didn't even want to play this stupid game, but I ask the first thing that comes to mind due to curiosity.

"All right. Do you always wear that much jewelry in a hot tub?"

My answer is a snort-laugh. "I'm on vacation, Charlie. On a superyacht! Do you know where Mason and I have vacationed for the last twenty years?"

I'm sure she's told me, but I just blink stupidly as I catch Rory returning from the flydeck bar. Even in my peripheral vision, I still see the slight tent a man's junk makes in such snug-fitting swimwear, making itself known at the front of his suit. I can't believe he wore a cock cage for an entire year. It's even more baffling now that I have a new perspective of who he is—a wealthy CEO. Granted, he was in college at the time, but how does one go from letting their cock be beholden to another person to being in such a position of power? Silently, I shame myself for such backward thinking, knowing that what we do for a living doesn't dictate our personalities. It's just…I guess I'm still new to contemplating the idea of giving someone that much power over my body. In my mind, I think I'd feel less confident and thus less likely to succeed in my professional endeavors. It's all so baffling to me.

"Disney World five times! Six Flags four times," Carmen rattles off animatedly.

"What did I miss?" Rory asks, slipping his lithe body back into the water.

"Charlie wanted to know why I'm all dolled up for the work cruise. I'm trying to explain to him that this is the first time I've ever been on a super yacht, so I'm damn well going to wear my diamonds if I feel like it."

"Fair enough." I hold my hands up in defeat, chuckling at her. "It was just a question. You're the one who wanted me to play your damn game."

She sends a splash my way, clearly not offended.

"I'm honored you dressed to impress," Rory quips. "What's that old saying? '*A garment needs only to please the wearer?*'" He smirks, taking a sip of his drink, and I catch myself in his gaze.

Is that a fucking cock cage joke? Because, if so, he already knows my truth. My garment does not please me.

"That's right," Carmen says smugly with a nod.

Great. I've created an alliance. Now, I'm not just the weird employee wearing a cock cage who let the CEO palm his balls and is no fun. And she wonders why I'm not having a good time on this trip.

"Are you going to give Rory shit now, too for being unglamorous, wearing just a chain with a key on it?" she asks.

What is she talking about now? I glance across the bubbling water at the man I've been avoiding looking at. He's still wearing that silver chain I glimpsed in his room yesterday, but now I can see it in its entirety. Dangling from the length over a light patch of dark curls is a little silver key.

"Is that his question?" Rory asks her. "I thought he wasn't playing."

"Ooh, you're right. It's my turn." Carmen perks up.

"Just for the record, I take no offense at being called unglamorous," he deadpans with a smirk.

He really isn't glamorous at all. He's always clean and well put together, but now that I know the extent of his wealth, I'm a bit surprised to find he doesn't flaunt it more in his appearance. The key on his chain isn't an adornment. It's just a plain metal key and isn't even affixed to an eyelet. It's almost like how guys keep one for a gym locker.

"That's not what I meant," Carmen chides, "but, fine, since we're on Charlie's boring topic," she pauses, casting an eye roll my way. Like I give a damn about this stupid game. "What's with the key? Does it unlock a safe full of pirate treasure on the yacht, or is it for something boring like life preservers?"

"Your priorities amaze me, Carmen." He chuckles, and I have to hold back a chuff at the way he's humoring her playful nature. Taking a deep inhale, he casts his eyes toward the darkening evening sky overhead in thought. "It's for something very special to me."

I don't understand the crypticism other than it seems like his MO. I couldn't care less about their sophomoric game, but that gets Carmen sitting up straight.

"Okay. Color me intrigued! Go on. Special how? Like a family heirloom?"

Rory lets out a soft laugh. "You already used your question."

"That was not an answer. And hardly a truth!"

"It wasn't a lie," he digresses.

Sighing dramatically, she rolls her eyes. "It's for the life preservers. Isn't it?"

"No. Those aren't locked up."

"Good to know, but you've got to give me more than that."

"Truth or Riddle, huh? Did we just level up?"

"What else have we got to do?" she challenges airily, turning her palms up.

I realize it's starting to look like I've been forgotten, so I plan my exit. I can just get out slowly and act like I'm going to head to the bar. Then I can slip back below deck while they're babbling.

Biting his lower lip in thought, Rory swirls his drink. "It's something I just had to have. The first time I saw it, I knew it was meant for me."

"Hmm. Was it expensive?" Carmen ventures.

"It's not something you can put a price on," he counters, fiddling with the little key between his thumb and index fingers.

"But you keep it locked up…" she hums in thought. "Are you afraid it could be stolen?"

"No, that's not possible. You can't steal something that's freely given."

I don't know why I haven't gotten out yet, other than I'm growing curious as to what the fuck he's talking about. Or maybe I'm just curious about how long it will take Carmen to give up on this stupid guessing game.

"So…it was a gift?"

"You could say that. It's certainly the greatest one I've ever received." His gaze flicks to mine as he adds, "It's a huge compliment to be given such a gift."

Letting go of the key, he lazily extends his arm across the edge of the tub. If I look away, I'll look like a guilty man who was recently seen in a cock cage, so I hold his stare even though it makes me want to squirm. He said those words earlier today when he was talking about cages. It feels like…he's taunting me.

"Can we see it?"

A hint of a smile plays at the corner of his mouth as he glances down at his drink. "No. Afraid not. I don't plan on ever sharing it with anyone."

I don't like the insinuations he's making about our conversation from earlier today. Something he won't share with anyone? Yeah,

I'm not being paranoid. He's fucking with me. Now, I am curious. What the fuck is that key for?

"Oh, I'm gonna figure this out. I'm not giving up," Carmen mumbles. "Is it on this yacht?"

"At the moment," he murmurs and then his eyes meet mine, "yes."

There's something heated about his stare. Combined with that one little word of affirmation he just uttered, it has me gasping. My lungs are suddenly heavy.

No. That's *not* what he means.

It can't be. He's just…fucking with me.

He's giving off his weirdo vibes again. I guess his professionalism at dinner was just a fluke.

"Hmm… Is it new? No, wait!" Carmen exclaims, acting like she's got a limit on the number of questions in this stupid riddle. "How long have you had it?"

"About…a week, I'd say." Bringing his drink to his lips, he continues to hold my gaze. "But if you want to get technical, you could say it's been *several* weeks."

A flood of heat washes over my skin. I'd like to think it's from sitting in this tub for too long, but I can't deny it's more likely from the feeling of Rory being one step ahead of me with his mind games. I find my gaze fixed on his key. I can't pull my eyes away as my heart pounds in my chest.

It's a small key. Very small. Small enough, it looks like it could fit my cage. And it's silver…the same color as my cage.

Fuck! No…

No. He…

How…

It *can't* be him.

He can probably have whoever he wants. Why would he go to a private club and cage some random guy in a…

I swallow against the dryness in my throat. I'm *not* some random guy, though, am I? I'm the one he gave the card to the club. He…he fucking knew I would be there.

Oh, God.

"Is it a work award?" Carmen asks curiously, like she thinks she's getting close to solving the riddle.

I find myself staring at his mouth as his gaze moves to her. "It has nothing to do with work, but…it's for a gift someone in my professional life offered me."

The words leave his lips, low and soft, creating a familiar tingling sensation in my balls. I'm hoping like hell it's just my paranoia that has me considering how his mouth seems like an exact perfect match to the one that brought me so much pleasure. A quiet panic creeps up my throat, making my hands tremble.

'A gift someone in my professional life offered me.'

The description both arouses and pisses me off. My cock is not a gift, but at the same time, I find myself blushing that someone would think of it as one. Who *is* this man? I've never heard any-one talk about another person in such endearing, intimate terms.

It's too much. I can't fucking take it. I have to get out of here before I plunge across this tub, snatch that key off his neck, and cause a scene in front of Carmen.

Turning, I push up and hop out of the tub in one quick move-ment. Landing on wobbly legs, I snag my towel and wrap it around my waist even as I move toward the steps, like it will hide my dirty secret that's not really a secret at all.

"Charlie? Where are you going?" Carmen yells.

"Cabin," I babble. "To my cabin. I…I'm done for the night. Goodnight."

Hustling down the stairs, every fiber of my being is vibrating as my wet feet hit each step, making me realize I forgot my damn flip flops. I'm not going back up there. I'll freaking murder him. I'll murder the damn CEO of my company and then have to explain in an interrogation room that I did it because he locked my cock up in a cage.

Because no matter how much I try to convince myself it wasn't him, I know it was. It was fucking Rory that breathed his hot breath on my cock and made me lose my mind so much that I begged for him to come back and do it again. I *did* offer myself to him, and now I don't know what to do about it.

CHAPTER 10

It feels like I stand for an eternity with my wet back pressed against the door to my cabin, trying not to hyperventilate. I'm caught in a montage of flashbacks—some from the club, others from my exchanges with Rory on the yacht.

How can someone who could deliver such out-of-this-world pleasure with just their mouth and limited touches be so…so…infuriating? So…not the right person for me? He's the fucking CEO.

Did he know it was me in that booth?

Gripping my skull, I pinch my eyes shut, trying to quell my emotions long enough to think clearly. How could he not have known it was me? There's no way it was just coincidence that he's wearing that fucking key. If I hadn't confided in him about my problem, would he have known I was the one who he'd caged?

"Listen to yourself, Charlie. You're being a fucking idiot."

He's a damn billionaire. Of course, he can get and do whatever and whoever he wants, while my three hundred bucks to the doorman didn't get me shit. He must have fucking planned on it from the second he gave me that card. Did that bald asshole tell him when I signed up to go to the club?

Was getting me on this cruise part of that plan?

But that explains nothing about how he said no one would put a cage on someone to be cruel. Or how he had plans for it.

Argh! None of this makes any sense. He could have just hit on me at that convention. He could have just talked to me through the portal. He could have… I don't know! Found any number of ways to communicate with me other than sneaking a cage onto my junk and leaving me in hell, and then surprising me on this cruise.

What is he playing at? Did he do this to anyone else on the cruise?

I'm pretty sure I'm the only gay employee on this ship. And pretty sure no one else looked like they were silently freaking out at dinner. But why me?

'It means they're so taken with you they can't bear the thought of sharing you with yourself or anyone else.'

The memory of his explanation has my throat going dry again and my pulse fluttering. *Taken with me?* How can he be taken with me when all he did was suck my cock? And if he's taken with me, this is sure as hell a shitty way of showing it.

The sound of a door closing next door makes my breath stop. He's back in his cabin.

I wait, heart pounding, as I listen. The bathroom door opens. I hear soft footsteps. The sink runs. Then nothing…

Wait. Do I hear…music?

Is he fucking kidding me? He's got nothing to say to me after all those cryptic messages up in the hot tub?

No fucking way. I don't care if he is the damn CEO. He's got some explaining to do.

Wrenching open my door, I glance down the corridor. The second I'm certain it's empty, I step out of my cabin and rush to Rory's door, rapping on it with determination.

I'm not some game to be played. He's not the CEO right now. He's just some strange asshole who either violated my trust in that club or took advantage of a secret I shared with him on this yacht and is messing with me. He's going to answer for it either way.

"Charlie…" A pleasant smile forms on his face as he opens the door. "How nice to see you again. You left so abruptly, I thought—"

I don't give him a chance to finish whatever bullshit he's trying to spew. Pressing my hand to his chest, which is still bare and warm from the hot tub, I push him back and make my way into his cabin.

Spinning around, I see that he's closing the door, unfazed by my forceful entry, which just pisses me off further. I grab hold of the door and slam it shut.

He's got his white towel wrapped around his waist and his chest…is bare. The chain and the key are gone. How fucking convenient.

"Cut the crap." Aiming my index finger at him, I keep my voice firm, but not so loud that I'm yelling. I don't think anyone's rooming near us, but I'm not going to take the chance of anything being overheard. "What the fuck are you up to?"

"What do you mean?"

I could put my fist in his face for how calmly he asks me that with a mask of confusion on his face. *'Down To Zero'* is playing softly through some speakers in the background. Its airy melody has me seeing red, knowing he was planning on relaxing in here like nothing happened while I was next door freaking the fuck out.

Poking him in the chest, I grit my teeth. "I *mean*…all that shit you said up there. About your fucking key. How you failed to tell me who you were when I confided in you yesterday. How you gave me that card to that fucking club. How I got invited on this cruise. Is there even a promotion or was it all just bullshit to get me here and fuck with me?"

His hand wraps around mine before I can give him another jab. His tight grip belies his calm. "Mm, you know more than you let on," he says, moving his body and my hand closer to me. "There is an opening for a promotion. I only invited the best candidates. Why? Did you want to work underneath me? Because I can tell you, while this heated little visit is entertaining, that's not the best way to go about it."

The fucker. He's doing it again. Him, his innuendos, and taunts. I'd fucking punch him if it wasn't for the sudden urge to get some distance between us.

Jerking my hand away, I'm surprised by how easily he lets it go.

Taking a step back, I plant my hands on my hips to let him know I mean business. Not the kind of fucking business he's talking about, though.

"It was you…at the club. Wasn't it?"

Tilting his head, he studies me. Seconds tick by, making my blood boil and my stomach squirm.

"Why? Did you want it to be?"

"This isn't funny."

Several weeks, he had said when Carmen asked him how long he'd had his *gift*. I never specified the timeframe that I'd been going to the club. The realization makes a lump form in my throat. I don't want it to have been him, and yet, if it was, that would solve my problem. I'd know I have the culprit right in front of me.

"Oh, Charlie," he murmurs, stepping toward me, his two more inches in height now seeming to make him tower over me. One of his hands plants on the wall next to my head. "Do you see me laughing?"

I can feel his body heat radiating off him. Feel his warm breath ghosting my face. It's now that I catch a hit of his spicy scent. It's mild, not the overwhelming kind from people who indulge in too much cologne. It's the same scent I remember from when I was in the room at the club—something mellow that made its way through the aroma of the leather panels. Fucking hell—it *was* him. I know it was.

"Give me the fucking key," I demand, but it comes out more like a harsh whisper.

His face falls in disappointment, and he clicks his tongue. "Are you sure that's what you want? Why you stormed in here all hot and bothered?"

His gaze moves down to my chest, which is now heaving more than I'd like to admit. I can feel splotches of color on my cheeks, too.

"Because…" he whispers, bringing his other hand up to my face. With the back of his knuckle, he drags it along the line of my jaw. "You begged so nicely for me to come back that day. And I was so happy to oblige." He leans in close to my ear. I gasp as I hear him inhale, like he's taking in my scent. And then his hot whisper hits the shell of my ear, "*Next week*. Remember?"

A burst of air rushes out of my lungs. Was I holding my breath? I can't move. Why can't I move? I should be shoving him the hell away from me, but it's like I'm paralyzed. That fucking whisper that once brought me so much joy is now keeping me prisoner in this spot. I'm trembling like I'm in the Arctic.

"G-get it off me," I manage. "Now. I…I want it off."

Pulling back, he drops his hands. The one that was on the wall drags softly down my bare arm before falling to his side as he turns away, sighing. "That's…so disappointing," he says sadly, moving toward the bed.

He pulls the towel from his hips, revealing that firm ass of his still clad in his Speedo. Bringing the terry cloth up to his head, he rubs at his damp hair, which has started curling on the ends.

"And here I thought we shared something…*special*."

I feel sick. And the damnedest thing about it is that I feel sick because I'd stupidly thought we'd shared something special, too. How fucking delusional was I? It was just a few orgasms, and I let them go to my head simply because they were *really good* orgasms. It wasn't special to him if he did this to me. He…he's just a sadist.

Sucking in a breath, I peel myself off the wall and take a step toward him. I can't look like a coward or some feeble creature just because he holds all the power right now. Maybe he thinks this is some coy sex game, but it's not. He's got me all wrong and needs to know I'm not playing.

"You tricked me and sucked me off. That's all it was. Now get this fucking contraption off me."

Turning around to face me, he frowns, and I'd swear his expression is pitying. He's still drying his hair like this isn't serious. I hold my ground, refusing to back away even though I'm not keen on being face to face with him after whatever the fuck just happened by the doorway.

"You're sure? You don't want to take a little more time to reconsider? You went to the club for an experience. Don't you think it might be worthwhile to see that experience all the way through?"

I fucking can't with him anymore. It's like talking to a boulder.

"Having my dick locked up for over a week wasn't the experience I asked for and you fucking know it. You've had your fun. Now get it the fuck off me. Game's over."

He stares at me for a beat, looking like I've…hurt his feelings, of all things. So bizarre. Everything about him is bizarre. I can't believe he's the one who made me feel the way I did. And I can't believe a part of me cares that I may have hurt his feelings. How is that possible?

"All right." He nods, finally.

I'm holding my breath again for some reason. Now that he's conceded and I no longer have to do battle, I don't know why I don't feel more relieved. Maybe it's because I still have this damn thing on my cock.

Yeah. I'll feel relieved once it's gone.

Warily, I watch him walk over to his desk chair and toss his towel over the back of it. Turning back around, he sets his hands on his lean hips and smiles.

"I take it that means you want to settle up for your violation now, then?"

"Violation? What are you talking about?"

Frowning, he moves to a sideboard and turns down the music. Opening a hatch, a small bar set up is revealed, and he proceeds to mix himself a drink.

"You broke the rules, Charlie. Three to be exact. *No talking. No soliciting. No breaching the barrier.* You violated the club agreement that you signed, and part of that agreement states that any violations are to be recompensed by a punishment of the club owner's choosing."

I didn't know it was possible to nearly swallow one's own tongue. As I stand here trying not to choke on my reaction to his new barrage of ridiculousness, I remember with clarity those absurd rules. I *did* talk to him. I asked him to come back, *soliciting*. *And* I stuck my fingers through the portal, *breaching the barrier*. But…what the hell did he care? Clearly, he enjoyed it!

"Yeah, I fucking doubt the club owner will care if we settle our differences outside the club. Cut the crap and just go get the key."

A soft chuckle has the muscles on his stomach rippling in a way I shouldn't notice as he brings his glass to his lips. Taking a sip, his eyes twinkle as he looks at me. Shrugging, a coy smile turns up at the corner of his mouth.

"I like to diversify my business holdings. What can I say? My father always said not to put all my eggs into one basket."

I think something in my brain actually detonates at this point. I've gone from not breathing to hyperventilating to fuming all in a matter of ten minutes. Of course, he's the fucking club owner. I fell right into this trap; hook, line, and sinker.

Clenching my fingers into fists, I try to keep my voice even. "Get it the fuck off me. Right now."

Setting his drink down, he places his hands on the sideboard and leans back on them. It elongates his torso, showing off every single bit of definition of his muscle tone. As if he couldn't look more smug, he crosses his long legs at the ankles and smiles.

"I'm glad you're willing to settle up so quickly. I do appreciate an admirable man who can admit his errors. Failure is only failure if you don't own up to it."

This prick. He has a screw loose. I swear. He's not going to make this easy for me, no matter what I say.

"What do you want?" I grit out each word slowly, so he knows just how unfreely I'm giving my compliance with this bullshit recompense.

There's that pitying look again. "You were new to the club, so I do sympathize with your predicament. You let your feelings get to you and forgot about the rules, I assume." A soft laugh. "I was there. I remember how…overpowering our exchange was."

Fuck him. Fuck…him. Don't let him goad you, Charlie.

"So…" he sighs, standing up and folding his arms. "How about I make this easy on you, since it was your first violation?"

First? He's fucking dreaming if he thinks I'm ever going back there.

"You came there for pleasure. I have to say, I still find it irresistibly adorable how particular and private you are, so I don't think a flogging on one of our group flogging nights would be an appropriate repayment for you."

Flogging? *Group* flogging? Is he fucking serious?

"I'd hate to see that special charm in you I found so precious to be tainted," he continues like this is some normal everyday conversation or, worse, a fucking business negotiation. "Club life isn't for everyone. You were brave to try it, and I admire that—a man who goes searching for ways to answer his hunger. So, in light of our…chemistry and your preference for privacy, I think I'll just ask you for what you came to the club for." Lifting his hand to his mouth, he whispers conspiratorially, "No need to send a customer away unsatisfied, even if he did manage to break all the rules in one session."

"What the fuck are you talking about?"

"You wanted to get off, Charlie," he says casually, walking past me toward the bed. "But you need someone else to do it for you."

How can he possibly know that? I didn't tell him. I've never told that to a soul.

"Am I wrong?" he asks when I don't answer.

"I can get off just fine on my own."

"Hm. I'd like to see that," he murmurs. "But, let me guess, it's not quite as fulfilling as when a stranger does it. When another person is involved."

"Yeah." I throw my hands up, turning around to face him. "Not at all like most of the other people on the planet. What an enigma I am," I huff. "Such a punishable offense."

Chuckling, he reaches into his nightstand drawer and pulls out a hairband. I watch his fingers comb through his long black hair, pulling it into a short ponytail at the back of his head. I have to say I prefer it left loose, but that's neither here nor there since what I'd really prefer is to have this conversation be over with.

"Not really," he agrees. "That's why I think helping you get what you came for will be the most fitting way of settling your debt." Leaning to the side, he pats the mattress. "I'm ready when you are."

I gape. Nothing he says should surprise me by now, but he can't possibly mean what I think he does.

"What?" I scoff.

"I'll consider your violations cleared if you can give us one little orgasm."

I laugh. Not a chuckle. Not a scoff, but a full-on belly laugh. And then I laugh some more.

"You're completely fucking mental, aren't you?"

"Three violations, Charlie," he says, turning back to his nightstand. "Settled by the very thing that you came to the club for. I think I'm being more than reasonable."

He is absolutely out of his damn mind. Now I do scoff. "Even if I agreed to settling up your bullshit violations, which would never hold up in court, there's just one problem—I couldn't fucking come in this stupid contraption even if I wanted to."

He turns back from his nightstand with a bottle of lube in his hands, making my breath catch. How does he keep doing that to me? I've never been so taken by surprise by someone this many times. I stare as he opens the cap and dribbles some on his index and middle fingers. The fucking gall on him, acting like I've already agreed.

"You should make sure to read contracts more thoroughly if you're considering the promotion. My legal team is very thorough, Charlie. You really don't strike me as the kind of person who'd want to go to court over your wrongdoings, but,"—he lets out a sigh—"if that's the way you prefer it, I'll respect your decision." Closing the bottle, he sets it back on the nightstand, looking at me so innocently, I almost want to laugh again.

Why does he have to keep saying my name like we're…close? It gives me gooseflesh each time he does. And what's with dangling the promotion in this fucked up conversation? Like I even have a chance or even want to work directly under him after this evening. And, no, I didn't read the stupid fine print on whatever I signed to get into his club. I still highly doubt that making someone come as compensation for a private club violation would even be entertained for a court hearing. He's right about one thing, however, I sure as hell am not going to push it that far. No one but us is going to know about this, if I can help it.

"I can't fucking come in this thing," I grit. "I…tried. Okay? Now, just go get the fucking key. I'll pay whatever you want."

I can't believe I'm falling for blackmail, but I'm so over this. And watching him rub the lube together with his other fingers has me trembling. Not in fear. I wish it were in fear. My body remembers the last time he had lube on his fingers and how good those fingers felt, making my cock twitch inside its barrier. What the hell is wrong with me?

"It makes me so sad that you believe that," he whispers tenderly. "I came in mine so many times. They were some of the best releases of my life. You're missing out, truly. That alone is worth a try; forget that it'd leave you even with the club. Think of it as a gift in exchange for the one you offered to me that day you called through the portal."

When he takes a step closer to me, my lungs lock up from a punch of unexplainable lust that hits me in the abdomen. Yeah, I asked him to come back, but…but that was before I knew it was him.

How can I be turned on right now? It's Rory. Rory, who locked me up and didn't tell me he was my CEO. Never mind that it's also Rory who has a magic mouth. He's still a dick.

Me and my stupid fucking kink of being aroused by the un-known. I've never been this turned on face to face with some-one, though. Dark clubs and dark bedrooms, maybe, but never when I have to hear and see a potential partner this much. Nev-er when I know the guy as much as I've come to know Rory. It's too…personal.

"I…I'm not…you…you're not fucking me," I manage, hating the building pressure in my already strained balls.

He just stares at me with that unnervingly calm gaze and more of what looks like sympathy. "It breaks my heart that you sound so adamant about that. I was so proud of you for being open enough to go to the club." He steps closer into my personal space. I tell myself I don't move as a show of defiance, but I honestly don't know if I can. That strange sensation of paralysis is settling in again from having him this close. "How about if I get the lights so it's closer to how you like it? Maybe you can be brave for me again."

Air floods my starved lungs again when he steps away. My brain scrambles for more expletives and arguments to talk sense to the most aggravating man in the world. Of course, I don't have to do this. It's absolutely ludicrous. Coming for him so I can clear my name at some club I never intend on returning to again? Utter bullshit. But I want this thing off my cock before this ship docks back on the main island and he disappears back to headquarters. I'm not stopping in there to beg him anymore to get me out of this. And this has been more than enough humiliation for one century. I don't even want to think about showing it to a doctor when I get back home.

The room goes dark except for a soft glow of moonlight coming from the gap around his cabin window's shade. It's a cruel effect, instantly making my flesh go tight at the knowledge I'm now alone in the dark, half-naked, with a willing, hot-blooded man. A man willing to do the very thing I once sought him out for. How does he know my undoing so well?

The way his quiet, calculating stare assessed me briefly at the convention months ago paints a completely different picture now. Did he know then? Is it even possible for someone to read another person so well?

"You'll like it, Charlie. Trust me. You trusted me before."

I try to reply to his confident assumption, but the words get caught in my throat as I track his shadowy figure moving back toward me. Blinking in the darkness, I clear my throat.

"I doubt it. And that was… before I knew you were a manipulative ass."

He makes a noise with his tongue. "I think you've got me all wrong. I saw that beautiful trembling cock of yours poke through the opening, trusting and eager. And then I could practically hear you clawing at the wall like you wanted to rip through it to come to the other side. God," he sighs. "Did you know I closed my eyes and imagined you doing just that? Running your fingers through my hair, guiding my head, thrusting into my mouth to give yourself what you wanted?"

Jesus, hell. How can he talk like that? I've never heard anyone talk like that. Not about me.

"And I'd have given it to you," he continues. "I knew you were special. At least…I thought you were. It was so sweet what you offered—begging me to be the one to come back rather than taking whoever we assigned to come to your room. I was touched. That's why I had that present made just for you. I wanted to return the compliment. I thought you'd like it."

I can almost see his face in the shadows now that my eyes have adjusted to the darkness. I can barely breathe as his heady words shower over me. Am I…responsible for some of this?

I *did* beg him to come back. And yesterday, up on the flydeck, I even admitted that I found it hot at first when he put the cage on me. Saying things like that to someone like Rory is like throwing a steak into a kennel of starving dogs. I can see that now.

My gaze scans all over the dark figure in front of me as my pulse kicks in my jugular. My nuts are so hard they're practically throbbing at this point and…and my freaking sphincter just clenched. It's an awkward reminder of how I was able to achieve that dry orgasm the other day. It's the only way I was even remotely able to get myself close to coming.

"And if…if this doesn't work," I choke out, sounding hoarse, wondering where his lubed-up fingers are right now. "You'll still take it off?"

"Oh, Charlie…you really don't pay attention to rules. After those intriguing stats you shut Gerald down with earlier, I'm surprised."

"Yeah, I fucking know I'm not getting a promotion, so just…just leave that out of this."

His heat grows hotter. I can make out the shape of his body right in front of me now.

A whisper tickles my ear, making me flinch in surprise at how close his face came without me realizing it. "Of course it's yours if you want it. You've been the most impressive performer for the past five years."

I…got the promotion? My heart flips in my chest, and my nerve endings light up even more.

"But no, my gift to you is an entirely separate matter from your violations," he adds, making my celebration come to an end.

Why the fuck am I even celebrating about a promotion? There's no way I can work for this guy after this.

"I thought…you said you'd clear my…violations."

I'm not sure why I'm repeating his asinine accusations that I don't even agree with. I'm also not sure why I'm whispering. Maybe because it's so damn dark in here. Maybe because I know what he wants, and he has lube on his fingers, and a mouth that gave me sensations I've never experienced before.

"Yes, and I will when you're ready to get on that bed, but," he pauses, letting out another of those sighs like he's being patient with a child, "I suppose I could compromise since you claim to have had such a bad experience with my gift."

I don't even want to ask him what he's talking about now. I think he gets off on it. So, I wait, a bundle of anxious nerves flooded by his potent scent now that my sight is gone.

"I'll tell you what, since you're a doubting Thomas about your ability to come in a cage. I'll make it even more worth your while. If you can let yourself go enough to get off, I'll give you those four numbers you're so certain you want."

Four numbers? The combination to the number lock on my cage?

"What about the key?" I demand, without thinking.

He chuckles then. The rumble of his chest tells me he's still mere inches away from me. "So greedy, just as I called it. You keep surprising me."

Fuck him. Fuck! Him! There's nothing greedy about me.

You know what? Fine. I'm not bantering with him anymore. If I get the code, I'll be home free. I can just pick the key lock and get the damn thing off on my own. Then, when I get home, I can make an anonymous call to the police about a risqué club that can in no way be legal.

Turning, I feel for the edge of the bed with my fingers. I lift my leg to slide my knee onto the mattress when a hand rests on my shoulder, giving me a start.

"Ah, ah. No wet trunks on my bed, please."

"Fucking ridiculous," I mutter, shucking them off and letting them drop to the floor.

Both knees on the bed, I realize I have no idea why he wants me on here or how I should sit. So, I wait. I wait in the uncomfortable silence. There's nothing but the darkness, Rory's scent, and my awareness of just how naked I am at the moment.

Something shifts in front of me. His shadowed frame drops. I hold my breath, waiting for more ridiculousness to come out of his mouth that will probably piss me off so much it will further slim the chances of me coming.

A gust of heat swaths my cock, shooting a tingle down my thighs, making all my leg hairs stand on end. The mattress dips on either side of my thighs. His hands resting there? He's…on his knees…breathing on me.

Oh, God. I think my dick just jumped and bumped into his lip.

Whiskers brush against the inside of my thigh as the breath moves in closer to the V of my groin. A satisfied sigh breezes over my tender flesh. I shudder so violently, my entire body quakes.

What is he doing? I thought maybe he meant he wanted me to get myself off. One more stupid assumption on my part. There's lube on his fingers for a reason. What's he going to do with those fingers? I'm supposed to be pissed off at him right now, but some weak part of me is hoping he'll massage around the cable again like he did yesterday. There's no way I'll come from that, but anything is better than the dormancy I've been a prisoner to.

"It's been a long week and a half for me, too," he whispers, letting his cheek slowly graze along the side of the cage.

And just like that, it feels like I'm actually back in that room. Just him and me, a dark barrier between us. No snarky taunts or coy games, just…sensation and desire. A punch of want pummels me in the gut and oozes lower, seeping toward my dick, down my legs, all the way to my toes. Little pings of electricity shoot to my balls when I feel his thumbs make little circles on the outsides of my calves. That's…that's new. Not something we could do with the panel between us, but…it's good. Way better than it should feel.

"You have no idea how much I wanted to be there last week."

He did?

Something nudges the top of my cage. I feel heat over the top of my cock. When he speaks again, I know without a doubt that it's his lips moving over the metal.

"My flight from New York was delayed. I was heartbroken. I had so many plans for this cock."

The air in the cabin seems ten times thicker than it was when I walked in. I'm practically gulping with each new breath at the thought of him trying to get back to me.

No. Not him. The guy who treated me so well. The guy he was before I found out he was Rory, I remind myself.

"You…c-could have sent a message."

His lips leave my cage. There's a soft rush of air as he rises. I feel his palm on the back of my shoulder, but I don't flinch this time. I'm too…malleable just from that reunion of his breath and my groin. So, I move before even realizing it when he urges me to turn.

"I know, but…I thought it might be a bit presumptuous of me, and part of the experience is the wait. I figured you should have the chance to see if you preferred pleasure elsewhere."

Elsewhere? How could I have gotten pleasure elsewhere?

"You went back, after all. Silas told me you stormed out, though. What happened?"

Silas? That must be the bald prick at the door.

A hand runs down my arm and stops at the underside of my wrist, but after the touch has left a trail of gooseflesh in its wake. "Hands on the bed, please," he whispers.

I'm about to argue when that warm palm lands on the small of my back, making me feel like warm molasses. Blinking stupidly like I'm in one of those Halloween fun houses, feeling for the walls, I touch my palms down to the bedding and tilt my head to track his movements as I try to keep my breathing under control.

"He…they laughed at me," I confess, hoping it hurts him to hear that as much as it hurt me to be left disappointed that night.

He doesn't deserve an orgasm from me, not after what he did. I want to shout at my body to stop responding to his little touches and grazes, but I'm determined to be the victor this time. I need those four fucking numbers, so he can't keep me under this strange spell he seems to cast whenever I'm around him.

I can't believe he was going to give me the promotion. Was he serious about that, or was he just telling me what I wanted to hear? He *knows* I've been the best performer for five years? That means he…noticed me. Noticed my work. I shouldn't take so much pride in that fact. It shouldn't make me feel so warm inside to have possibly been on his radar for so long.

"It was horrible," I mumble.

I'm not sure if I do it to make him feel bad or if the words just tumble out like he's opened some fountain of truth in me with his hot breath and the cloak of darkness.

His palm slides across the small of my back. His hand is a little rough, but his touch is gentle. It's oddly soothing and yet lights my flesh on fire at the same time. It doesn't stop, though. The mattress dips behind me and his palm continues over the curve of my ass and down the outside of my thigh.

I suck in a breath when I feel the full weight of him on the bed. His leg hair brushes against my skin, and I knead the comforter in anticipation.

What is he doing back there? I told him he's not fucking me, and for some reason, despite all his mind games, I believe he'd actually respect that.

His leg presses against the inside of mine, nudging mine outward. On instinct, I move it. His other one brushes over the back of my other calf, painting a clear picture of him settling between my legs.

Jesus. Thank God he can't see my exposed ass. I've never shown that view to anyone, too mortified of feeling so…open.

"I'm sorry, Charlie."

His other hand connects with my hip, the same light touch. The same soothing warmth. He glides it down the outside of my thigh and then runs it back up in unison with his other hand until they both stop on the top of my ass.

The touch and the apology unlock something in my breathing, allowing my air to come more freely. It's a modicum of the comfort I've yearned so much for over the last week and a half. It grips my heart with a squeeze of sadness that has me nearly wanting to cry.

How bizarre is that? It has to be this fucking cage. It's plagued my emotions for far too long.

His hands move again, trailing down the back of my thighs this time. I'm about to squirm and tell him I'll need much more than that if I have the slightest chance of coming. One of his hands slips in between my legs, though. His palm glides over the underside of my balls, stealing my breath once again.

"Truly…I am," he whispers, his lips dusting the flesh at the small of my back.

I feel those lubed fingers now as they delicately start to trace the circumference of the cage's cable. But that's not the worst of it. A soft, wet kiss touches my skin right above the cleft in my ass. I shudder so hard that there's no way he didn't feel it against his lips.

"I wouldn't have laughed," he murmurs, moving his mouth to my right cheek and placing another kiss there.

I…he never said anything about…about kissing. No one's ever…kissed my ass. I don't know what to think. It's not something I ever thought I'd like, but as his fingers slink up the underside of my cage in a gentle massage of my tender flesh, the combination seems to work. I can feel blood pulsing to my shaft, making the confines even smaller now. All the while, his palm brushes my sac. It forces an awareness over me of just how heavy it feels right now. I do need to come. Need to, despite anything to do with being granted four little numbers. I know I'm supposed to be pissed off right now, but for the love of God, if he can actually make me come, I don't think I'd be mad about it.

I grunt, suddenly frustrated. All that this stroking and the unexpected kisses to my ass are doing is making me harder. It's not like either of us could work my cock right now.

"What is it, handsome?"

My face blooms with heat over the unsolicited compliment. Does he actually think I'm handsome?

Fuck. Focus, Charlie.

"I…I can't come. This isn't going to work."

His hand retreats from between my legs. I feel the loss instantly, even though I basically requested it. All he's doing is getting me hot and bothered. I had no problem feeling like that already without his hands on me. If he's fucking with me again so he can get away without giving me the damn combination, I'm going to resort to physical violence.

The next thing I know, his chest presses against my back, a blanket of fleshy heat. His nipples flattened against the back of my ribs, his soft chest hair. His arms cage the outsides of mine and the fabric of his Speedo brushes the back of my ass.

Right at the center of my seam, something thick and solid nestles against me behind that spandex fabric. He's hard. So hard it has me sucking in a breath.

His lips brush against the back of my ear and soothe, "Hey, hey…*shhh*. Patience. We've just started." When his nose makes a playful nudge against the skin behind my ear, I gasp like a damn virgin. "I'm not going to let you down again. I promise."

He lifts one of his hands off the mattress. I feel it on my chest and wonder if he can tell how fast my heart is beating. It doesn't linger long, though, instead moving slowly down my stomach and to my abs.

I've never felt so surrounded by another person. I'm used to blow jobs or topping someone from behind against a wall. Is this what it feels like for a bottom when you fold yourself over them? It provides its own unique sense of fulfillment. So I stay put, comforted by the promise of not being let down again, which I probably shouldn't have any faith in.

With this full-body blanket hug, complete with his dick still nestled in my seam, I'm reminded of the deep exploration I made with my fingers earlier in the week when I was trying to get off. It was the wrong memory to recall. My hole spasms and my ass clenches.

I freeze. There's no way he didn't feel that. I don't dare move a muscle, not even when he moves back.

His hips retreat, bringing me both relief and further convincing me I'm never going to come. A moment later, his hands are back on my ass, though. They glide back down the outsides of my thighs. I'm about to roll my eyes and tell him that starting back at square one won't produce the results we both want. Ass play isn't my thing, and he's locked up the one place that always produces results. I can't believe I even got into this position for someone, let alone allowed everything to happen so far that has.

I'm quickly learning, however, that Rory is a master of the bait and switch. As soon as I fixate too long on or panic about one thing, it's like he knows and changes tactics. His lips dust the back of my ass cheek this time, very, *very* close to my cleft.

"Are you ready?" he murmurs, sliding his hands around my waist and down to the juncture of my hips.

I let loose some unintelligible sound, frozen again. He's…not going to… Is he?

It starts with another kiss. A soft, innocent kiss near the seam of my ass. What follows is a mapping of its entire height all the way up to the top of my cleft. Something wet swirls a circle over the vertebrae right above my ass, leaving me gasping in a rush of shivers. And then…he sucks the sensitive skin there. Sucks on it!

My eyes may have just crossed. It's ticklish, and my toes curl as more blood pumps to my already strained balls.

H-how…how is that…an erogenous spot?

"Mmm," he hums.

Did I shudder again? Or make some embarrassing noise? What was the hum for?

I don't have time to analyze it. He moves lower with that wicked mouth of his. Straight down.

I'm honestly concerned for my brain because of how many times I've held my breath tonight. When his hot breath ghosts slowly down the length of my seam, though, I can neither get any air to come in nor out of my lungs.

He pauses at my taint. If someone dropped a pin, I'd hear it. I wait, suspended in place by those hands that are stroking my juncture, making my cock bob with each drag of his fingertips. Wet and soft…I feel it first at the tender flesh behind my balls.

"Uhn!" I bark out a groan and jolt against his hands when his tongue paves a path between my cheeks.

It stops right on my ring and withdraws, allowing me to suck in a gulp of air. And then…there are lips.

Holy hell, I think I just squeaked or…squawked. Whatever it was, I don't want to repeat it. He's…kissing my pucker. *Kissing…* as in repeatedly.

All I can do is hang my head and pinch my eyes closed, trying to will my elbows to bend so I can move away. But they won't budge. I'm locked in place, vibrating from head to toe like my freaking electric shaver. Literally, I'm quaking. Each brush of his lips, each little suckle, pulls needy whimpers from my mouth.

Fuck. This is so embarrassing, but I'm helpless to stop my reactions.

Worse yet, I can feel my heartbeat in my balls like a pounding migraine headache. *Thump, thump! Thump, thump!* It's too much. Too much pressure. No wonder I can't breathe. I'm going to pass out from all my blood being forced into my nuts with nowhere for it to go. Some of it must have made it through the cable to my cock, though, because it's practically arced inside the cage, pushed to the limit against the restraints of the metal. I'm going to have indentations of the rings on it if I ever get out of this thing.

I hear a slurping sound and then another of Rory's satisfied hums as he continues his onslaught of filthy kisses. They're getting filthier, open-mouthed, with laps and swirls of his tongue around my circumference. I shout inside my head for my body to move, to pull away before I pass out, but nothing happens. Only that involuntary quivering and the humiliating noises I'm making.

"P-please… Rory," I stammer. "*Please*."

The rest of my plea won't form on my lips. I'm lucky I even got that much out.

"What do you need, Charlie?" His words vibrate against my hole.

His thumbs dig into the meat of my hips, thrusting me back against his mouth as soon as the words are out. This time, it's not his lips that greet me, but the tip of a slippery, wet tongue.

"T-to come. *Ineedtocome*. N-now!"

The flexible muscle presses forward, slipping its way past my ring. It's soft and foreign, warm. So unlike how my finger felt. I gasp at the way it fits with ease, expanding me ever so slightly, filling me when he dives so deep, I can feel his jaw press against my taint.

I'm so confused. Completely bewildered. That's not what I meant, but he didn't ask what I *wanted*, rather what I *needed*. I *wanted* to stop before I passed out. What I *need* is entirely different, and I answered truthfully.

I have a tongue in my ass. Rory's tongue. With each slide and wicked lick inside my channel, a shiver shoots up my spine and makes my legs quake with more fervor. The surreal part is that it seems like I've reached a higher plane. One where I think it might actually be possible for me to come. Either that or passing out is truly more imminent than before.

Groaning, I reach for my cock on instinct, but whimper when my palm connects with the metal of the cage. I settle for making tiny strokes to my flesh between the rings with my thumb. It's not enough, though. With each of Rory's delves inside me, he grazes my prostate, but it's just a tease. Light tickles from that soft tongue that aren't enough pressure. I have no idea how much is enough pressure on my prostate to make me come in a cage, but intuition tells me if I could just get a little more, I might be able to get myself out of this blissful misery that's turned me into a babbling mess.

I thrust back without thinking. His jaw stabs me below my entrance, making it clear I essentially just jacked him in the face with my taint. But it's not enough. All it produced was another of those teasing grazes to my gland. I groan in misery. If I had my razor, maybe the combination of the pressure and the vibration would be enough. God, I'm never going to come again. Am I?

"I can't." The words come out weepy.

His tongue retracts, pulling another sobbing sound from my lips. I hate this. I hate my life. I hate my cock. Hate my prostate. Hate my kink that got me into this mess.

Rory's palm comes up and rubs a circle over my back. "Don't worry, handsome. I've got you."

I dangle on that reassurance, an odd bit of comfort. There's a *flick* sound, and then cool liquid dribbles down my seam. It's a rude awakening to the hot, wet heat that was just there. I suck in a breath through my teeth and shiver.

"Sorry," he murmurs as two fingers swoop down between my cheeks, catching the liquid like he's coating them. "If we were at my house in Northwest Heights, I'd have used my Chinese oil warmer," he says casually, turning his hand and running two fingertips up to my ring. "I can set it to body temperature, so the oil feels perfect when you get it inside you."

Inside you? The words have my gland reverberating in anticipation even as a sliver of worry runs down my spine. I think I knew that was his plan the second he coated his fingers earlier, but my pride opted for convenient denial.

Something about him makes me want to…try new things. I think it's the real reason he ruffles me. And he does just that, slipping his index finger through my ring without any warning.

I'll give him credit—he does it slowly, gently. But it's still a shock. He's only the second person besides me to have put a finger inside me.

"Breathe," he whispers, rubbing my side with his other hand.

I listen. I don't like that I listen so freely. How did we get to this place where I do what he asks me to and…enjoy it?

I make to protest, some kind of sound to let him know that he's not in charge of me, but all that comes out is a moan. When his finger rubs my gland, the moan unfolds into something deeper and throatier. He traces around that bundle of nerves inside me, stealing my breath. It sends a wave of heat down my legs, a telling sign that usually happens right before I come. But this time…it doesn't come. *I* don't come.

I groan in frustration. What is wrong with me? He said he came in a cage plenty of times. Am I broken?

"So greedy," he whispers, leaning over me and planting a hand on the bed next to mine.

I turn my head in shame. As if this couldn't have gotten any worse.

His lips dust my ear, and he makes a chiding sound. "No, don't be embarrassed. I love it. I love how greedy you are."

There's pressure on my ring, expanding it. I blink through the darkness, trying to make sense of the change. The next thing I know, I'm fuller. Full of Rory's fingers. He added a second and…it should not be so satisfying.

When my college fuckbuddy suggested we try switching once, it sold me on the idea that ass play was not my thing. He'd unceremoniously spit on my hole and then tried nudging his cockhead slowly inside. My nerves and being exposed like that for the first time were already enough, but the burn that ensued told me pleasure was *not* going to be the outcome, so I called it off.

Maybe I wasn't relaxed enough. Maybe he was just the wrong person, or I wasn't ready. I don't understand how Rory can be the right person, and I certainly wouldn't say I was ready now, having thought nothing of it in all these years. However, I'm suddenly aware of just how relaxed I am. Despite all my verbal and internal bitching, I…there's something about Rory. Something I don't exactly hate. His voice, his gentle, warm touches—they calm my body into a pliable mess of compliance. My cynical mind may not trust him, but my body certainly seems to.

I stay poised on my hands and knees, immobile. Mouth hanging open, my jaw has lost the ability to move. A series of moans and hot breaths flood past my lips as he fucks me with those two slippery fingers, tapping my gland on each insertion.

Another wave of heat doubles down, rippling over the last. My God, it feels like my lower half is on fire. My cock starts bobbing like it's at rave. My balls feel like granite. I'm pretty sure they're going to crack.

This is it. The moment I finally pass out. I cry out a roar of anguish, at least grateful that I'll meet the darkness in this haze of unrelenting bliss. Rory's lips attack the place behind my ear, sucking violently at the tender skin there as he groans with me. It unlocks something deep in my groin, right behind my nuts, as the blackness is peppered with tiny spots of light in my vision.

I come.

I come hard and ferociously, convulsing, with no control over my limbs. The mattress shakes, and all the while, his fingers remain dedicated, stuffed inside me, massaging my gland.

My back arches, and I lean into Rory's mouth like a victim drunk on a vampire's kiss. Smatterings of my release sprinkle my hand and my knees. My weight floats away like ashes in the wind until there's nothing left but the familiar pull of my cage on my cock. I'm as light as the air, all my worldly troubles wiped from my mind, floating on an ethereal cloud of rapture.

My bones give way, and I fall, but it's in slow motion. I'm still shuddering through every ripple coursing through me. My cock is still pulsing out the pent-up release its been denied. And I'm... warm. So comfortably warm.

Something brushes my arm. Through my haze, I realize it's Rory's thumb. His chest is pressed against my back. I'm on my side and he's cradling me from behind, one arm acting as a pillow underneath my head.

"I've got you," he soothes.

A humbling self-awareness pricks my blissful bubble like a needle. Did he lower me to the bed? How long have I been lying here moaning and gasping while he held me?

For some reason, I think of that time when I was fourteen and my brother Brett burst in on me in the bathroom where I was jerking off. I'd been looking at a model in an issue of Men's Health—*a male model.* I knocked the magazine off the counter in time so that he didn't see what was helping me get off, but I still couldn't stand the sound of his laughter or the razzing he and my other brothers gave me after he ratted me out. While my current mortification feels close to that, I still don't move. Because... it also feels nice being held after that emotional upheaval, and Rory...well, like he said, he's not laughing. I have a feeling that if I moved, making an awkward attempt to leave, his teasing would resurface, though. I'm not sure how I feel about how it means he seems most happy when I'm completely undone and vulnerable.

I don't have to dwell on it much longer because he pulls away. Wait. Did I do something wrong?

A dim light flickers on near the headboard, a rude glow snuffing out the darkness. I swallow at the sight of the mess in front of me on his comforter. It's what he wanted. It's what *I* wanted, but... damn. The amount of evidence is damning considering the fuss I made.

Suddenly, he's in front of me. Kneeling on the floor, he drags his towel over my knees and then my stomach. My face is burning. I didn't imagine him to be an aftercare type of person. No one's cleaned me up before, and I'm at odds over how to act. Awkwardly, I rise on one elbow and silently reach for the towel to let him know I'm a big boy who can take care of myself, but then he grips the cage and starts to dab at the dribbles running down my cock. It's too much. Just like everything else with him.

"I...I can do that," I stammer, grabbing the towel and backing away.

He releases it, watching me with curious eyes. They look darker than usual, as though they're full of hunger and wonder, but I tell myself it's my imagination. I rise on wobbly legs. The carpeting is a cruel reminder that I've fallen back to earth. I'm still trembling from head to toe. I don't know how I'll even be able to walk back to my room.

What do I do now? My debt is settled. Because now that my balls are drained and my head is clearing, I remember that's why we did what we just did—to clear my violations. I glance at the door, knowing it's how I can flee this awkwardness.

When I look back at Rory, his expression has fallen. For someone who always appears so confident and self-assured, the sad grace in his features leaves me in awe with a pang of guilt. I have no reason to feel like I've let him down. I gave him more than I ever intended to give when I stormed in here a while ago.

Wrapping the towel haphazardly around my waist, I rush toward the door. There's too much light, too much weight from his gaze, too much satiation in my exhausted limbs, too much tenderness to my spent cock. I have neither the fortitude nor emotional capacity to deal with any more of his banter or riddles right now if he starts up again.

"Charlie…" he calls when I'm mere feet from the door.

And like a programmed robot, I stop. Why did I stop? Move, Charlie. Leave!

"You're forgetting something."

I turn, ready to do battle and tell him I'm not in the mood for any more of his tricks, but I find him taking a knee in front of me. His hands go to the place where I tucked the towel around my hips.

Shit. It's his towel. His towel, soiled with my release.

I stand numbly as he pulls it away. He's already seen everything. What do I care if he sees it again?

When his hands let go of it and reach for my cage, my spine goes rigid. Is he…going to suck me off over the cage? A zap of electricity snakes up my spine at the thought, even though I'm so drained I doubt I could come again.

But then his fingers lift the cage, and he leans in. The metal jostles, and I hear a clicking noise. Then another click. And another.

The combination.

How could I have forgotten about that? It was the reason I got on that bed in the first place.

His hands move to the towel in my grasp again. I stare dumbly as he tucks it back in place around my hips. He rises. Our gazes lock, and it's like staring down into a dark well. He's never been this speechless before. Part of me wants to know what unspoken words he's holding back. Is it another game? Another trick? He looks…different now, though. Like a smoke screen has cleared. I must be dreaming. It's wishful thinking I didn't even wish for. Why am I not gone yet? I am so out of my element here.

When his lips part, that's all it takes to spike my fear enough that I move. I cannot compete with Rory McDonnell. He left me clawing at a wall several times and now a blubbering mess in a puddle of my own cum on his bed. I don't stand a chance of surviving with a shred of dignity if I tangle with him any further.

Wrenching the door handle open, I bolt out into the corridor. It's not until I'm safely back in my cabin that I realize I don't even have my shorts, and I've just stolen his towel. Leaning against my closed door, I pant like I ran a marathon.

I just let the CEO lick and finger my ass until I came to the point of nonsense, *and* I enjoyed it. And I think…he offered me the promotion.

What the fuck just happened?

CHAPTER 11

The shuttle bus pulls away from the beach, leaving me with a foreboding wariness in my gut. We're far from civilization for the mandatory closing activities that were listed on the flyer I found slipped underneath my cabin door this morning. It's going to be a long day with nowhere to hide unless I sneak off into a palm grove.

I doubt anyone else who read that flyer opened their cabin door to find their swim trunks neatly folded in the corridor, along with their flip-flops. It was a brutal reminder of my shameful behavior last night after I'd spent a good hour convincing myself to forget it ever happened as I got ready for the day. Did Rory put them there, or did he tell one of his stewards to do it for him?

Wading through the white sand, I refuse to help the gaggle of others who are assisting Rory in setting up a large pop-up tent. My cage swings against my thighs with each step as I head toward Niel and Gerald, who look to be trying to make sense of how to erect a volleyball net. I had the gumption to look at the combination Rory entered on the number lock last night before I went to bed. Thank goodness. Who knows if I would have nudged a number in my sleep and ruined any chance of remembering the combo. My weak attempt at picking the key lock this morning was another story entirely. I was too distracted by the pleasant sensitivity in my ass and the memory of lips and fingers ghosting my cock to concentrate. Either that or I'm just shit at picking locks.

Wrapping a sock around my cage seemed like a logical solution to avoiding its form being seen through the pair of trunks I put on today for this mandatory fun. Never mind that it's hot as fuck and my dick now feels like it's suffocating. I probably look incredibly well-endowed to boot, so if someone hadn't looked before, they'll certainly notice now.

Fuck it. That's better than them seeing a cage imprint through my trunks. I don't plan on partaking in any of the activities today if I have anything to say about it, though. The coolers stacked up near where they're setting up the tent have enough liquor in them that I think I know where I'll find my enjoyment today.

An hour passes while everyone employs themselves, setting up all the crap Rory's crew loaded into one of the shuttle vans. I spend it popping up folding chairs and staking down the volleyball net, keeping a keen eye on Rory. It's an hour of sneaky glances that leave me realizing he hasn't once looked in my direction. Does he even know I'm here?

He's been busy erecting the tent, setting up folding tables for a makeshift buffet, and hauling the stack of coolers underneath the canopy. Laughing and smiling, he directed each of his helpers with sunshine-y professionalism. All my snooping has done is show me he isn't afraid of manual labor and has an admirable level of fitness for a billionaire. How can last night *not* be the foremost thing on his mind right now?

Did he get himself off after I left? I'm shocked he never asked for anything for himself, especially after I felt how hard he was when he pressed up against me. My face heats, remembering his words.

'I love it. I love how greedy you are.'

How can he be perfectly okay with how wanton I was? Both last night and at the club? At the club, I stuck my cock through a portal and he did all the work, even then. So far, I've taken and not given anything. Who can be happy being on the opposite side of an exchange like that? I don't understand.

"Charlie, are you in?"

Shaking myself from thoughts that I have no business thinking in front of my co-workers, I find Niel tossing a volleyball at me. I catch it just as it hits my chest and find all the salespeople and Rory milling around the volleyball net.

"Uh...no. You guys go ahead." I toss the ball back, but Niel chucks it right back at me.

"Let me rephrase that," he laughs, flipping his sunglasses down from his head. "You're first up to serve. There are only twelve of us, and we need six on each team."

There aren't twelve of us. There are thirteen if you count Rory, who's lost his flip-flops and his freaking tank top, like he's planning on partaking in the match *Baywatch* style. There's a chain around his neck—*the* chain. The chain with *the key*. I officially fucking hate him again.

As I count people and piece together my protest to give to Niel, I spot Salvador lounging in one of the folding chairs near the tent. Salvador, a salesman from one of the eastern regions. Salvador who has a fucking boot on his foot because he broke his ankle right before the cruise.

Son of a bitch.

It would be a lie if I said I wasn't getting into the match. At least half of my brain cells have. With each jump Rory makes, however, his key lofts into the air before bouncing back down on his chest, leaving me distracted. When we rotate and he's bent over in front of me, I pay way too much attention to the shallow dent between the cheeks of his concrete ass in yet another Speedo. The few serves I've managed not to fuck up have gotten me a slap on the shoulder, so unlike his tender touches last night.

This is hell. This is sweaty-sock-around-my-caged-cock hell. If he'd just take those stupid sunglasses off, maybe I could get some reassurance if I saw an indication of something in his eyes.

Like what, idiot? I chide myself. The man never flusters. You just want to look into his eyes. Admit it.

The ball catapults right toward me as Niel yells. I dive in an attempt to punt it back over the net, but it's in vain. My chest hits the sand, knocking the wind out of me. My cage smashes into my stomach, and I slide. I close my mouth in time so that I at least don't eat a cup of sand.

"Fuck," I mutter as my teammates groan at my failure.

"Damn it, Charlie. Now we're tied," Niel laments.

Rising, I dust my face and chest off, wishing I could tell Niel where to shove his sudden thirst for victory. This is so fucking stupid. Mandatory fun isn't supposed to be fun. Everyone knows that.

I don't know why he drank the Kool-Aid, but at least I did my part in reminding him of the reality.

I turn back to my place in the front row before the net again. Rory's fist taps me on the shoulder, giving me a start to find him so close.

"I think you dropped this."

Fuck! Fucking, fucking, fuck!

I yank my sweaty sock out of his hand and turn my back to him in a flash, my face going up in flames. Tucking the damp cotton into the front of my waistband, I want the sand to open up and swallow me.

The play starts before I have time to dwell on my newest humiliation. Rory sets up Carmen, who spikes the ball beautifully between two players on the other team, leaving the ball back in our court.

We rotate into our positions as Niel tosses me the ball. One serve and this shitshow can end. I can grab a drink and go drown myself in the ocean. There's a slap on my ass as I get my footing for my turn to serve. It sends a delicious shudder through me that goes straight to my cock.

"You got this, Charlie."

I blink at Rory, shocked that he put a hand on me in front of everyone else. It's not the first ass slap I've seen today. It's just the first one I've felt. A bizarre sensation tickles my insides.

'I knew you were special.'

The memory of those sultry words dances in my ears like a flirty marionette. And yet, as I stand here having a moment, he's already in his stance, hunched over, hands on his shapely thighs like nothing just happened.

"Come on, Charlie. I'm hungry," Carmen whines.

Great. I'm the klutz who's now holding up the game. Sucking in a breath, I shake the thoughts away and toss the ball. Jumping, I rear my arm back to connect. The strangest thing happens. An image of Rory spanking my naked ass while I kneel obediently for him on his bed flashes through my mind just as the ball is inches from my palm. I choke, literally and figuratively.

The ball curls sloppily off my fingertips and lobs in a pathetic arc, nicking the top of the net without clearing it. A host of grumbles erupts from my teammates while the other side cheers, knowing they now hold a chance at the winning serve.

Rory claps in quick succession, addressing the rest of our teammates. "It's all right. It's all right. We've got this."

But we don't '*got this*' because, as Gerald makes a shitty set-up for someone to spike after the other team served the ball to our side, I realize too late that his shitty set-up sent the ball in my direction. I was still blinking at Rory, trying to decide if he was sticking up for me when the ball smokes me in the forehead.

The other team erupts in cheers. Mine curse and moan unsportsmanlike oaths.

"Jesus, Charlie," Gerald sneers. "We should have asked Salvador to play instead."

I catch Rory looking at me then. He takes a step forward, making me forget about the throbbing sensation above my eyebrow, but Carmen beats him to it.

"Gerald, it was a beach match, not the Olympics. Get over yourself." Reaching out, she dusts some sand from my forehead, bringing me back to the present. "Are you okay? What's with you today?"

Backing away, I shake off her mothering. "Too much sun, I guess," I mutter.

Nodding, she loops an arm through mine and urges me toward the food tent. "Come on. Let's get some lunch. I bet you'll feel better with some food in your stomach."

I glance around for Rory, but he's already in the gaggle of the other team, congratulating them on their win. Was he actually going to say something to me? Was he concerned that I got pelted in the face? Why do I want him to have wanted to say something? It was just a ball to the face. I'm fine. It's not like this is an appropriate place to comment on anything that happened last night.

The afternoon drags on with more misery. I shove food in my mouth in silence, sitting in a circle of folding chairs with some of the sales reps while Rory's laughter floats across the beach as he speaks to everyone but me.

Unable to stand anymore of the mundane chit chat, I stomp off to the ocean and swim until my legs cramp, still spent from the powerful release last night. By the time I return to the beach, the sun is setting, and someone's started a bonfire. Just my luck that everyone has seemed to congregate around it, including Rory.

"There he is," he enthuses, granting me a rare smile.

My stomach flips. I just nod and continue drying myself as I find a free chair. Collecting my sandy tank top, I yank it over my head and accept the bottle of beer that Carmen hands me. If I can't avoid feeling self-conscious, I can at least numb it with some liquor for whatever fuckery is next.

Rory proceeds to thank all of us for our hard work and dedication to the company. He tells us how much fun he's had being on this cruise and getting to know us. I try not to snort, wondering how much of that declaration of fun has to do with him fingering my gland last night. He informs us he'll be sending out an offer packet for a promotion to one lucky candidate in the next week, which gets him a few gasps and squeals of joy. And then he turns up the music and takes a chair on the opposite side of the bonfire, preventing me from seeing him through the heat of the blaze.

Am I the lucky candidate? I know what he said last night, but did he mean it? And do I even want to be?

In the grand scheme of things, I know I shouldn't even be worrying about it. I should be counting the minutes until we get back to the ship so I can work on picking the lock on my cage, not drowning in curiosity over whether I'm the apple of Rory McDonnell's professional eye. The longer I sit amidst the merriment of my co-workers, however, the deeper my agitation grows. Each time I glimpse Rory's face across the firelight, each time I spot his smiling lips, my nuts flutter. One drink turns to three and then four, trying to silence the memories of the pleasant sensations in my ass. I try to catch what Carmen and the others are saying. I even throw out a laugh every now and then, so I look like I'm paying attention. Each time I see Rory's index and middle finger wrapped around his beer bottle, however, I find myself having to stifle little noises of…want.

'What do you need?'

I don't *need* him. I don't. Except that means this unexplainable pull I'm feeling is, in fact, want. How can I want such a man now that I know him? I let him crack me open and do things I never thought I would do. He made me like things I never intended to like. I've never spent so much headspace on anyone I've hooked up with, so what is the deal? Is it just his unique brand of foreplay and methods that have me stuck on him?

Maybe I'm just learning a lesson I never considered before—that it's possible to like how someone can make you feel, even if you don't like that person. Attraction has always just been physical for me, so it makes sense. Maybe when I get home and I'm not forced to look at him anymore, I'll be free of all these surprising urges. I still can't believe I'm attracted to someone I've had to have so much face-to-face contact and conversation with. Maybe my tastes are changing with age.

By the time the shuttle vans show up and we load back into them, I'm at my limit of being ignored. I'm even more at my limit of being aggravated about being ignored. What the fuck do I care if he hasn't looked at me or talked to me all day? I've got the combination. That's all I really needed.

I mumble my goodnights to Carmen, Niel, and the others when we arrive back on the yacht. Tromping my way down the corridor to my cabin, my limbs are heavy from the beer I sulked over. It emphasizes the weight at my groin, a cruel reminder of my attachment to the man who occupies the next cabin. Scanning my room, I find the tweezers where I tossed them to the floor this morning and fetch them.

Flopping down on my bed, I shove the waistband of my trunks down and scoot back against the pillows. It's time to be rid of this thing once and for all.

Inserting the end of the tweezers into the keyhole, I press them against the locking mechanism. Or, at least, what I think is the locking mechanism. I'm going to take a lock picking course after all this is over, I swear.

Gripping the section where the sac cable slides into the hollow metal frame on the underside of the cage, I wiggle it back and forth, hoping it will help the mechanism inside give way. Each tug I make to the cable applies pressure to my trapped balls, tugging grunts from my lips.

"This is such bullshit," I mutter, shifting on the bed and widening my legs.

Just as I shift my cage to go at the keyhole from a different angle, I hear commotion next door. The sound of pipes running filters through the walls. The droning of water falling has me straightening.

Rory's back, and he must be in the shower. Well, good for him. I'm glad one of us can relax after a long day under the sun at the beach, and the world's most humiliating volleyball match.

Shaking my head, I hunch over again and line up the tweezers. I hope he's in there soaping himself up and thinking about how he can't toy with me anymore.

Yeah, he's probably plotting his next visit to his club. Maybe someone else caught his eye, and he's already got another custom cage being designed for them. It's not impossible. The more I think about how possible it is, the more my stomach turns.

"Ouch! Damn it!"

The tweezers fall from my hand after they slip and jab me in the cock. Fuck that hurt! I check for blood, but they didn't pierce my skin, just grazed it.

Fucking Rory. This fucking ship. What do I care if he didn't bat an eye at me all day and how '*special*' he supposedly thinks I am? If I were so special, he'd be over here knocking on my door, not ignoring me and taking the world's longest shower like he's planning on plopping into bed for a relaxing night of sleep afterward.

I palm my tweezers again and rub the red mark on my cock, wincing. This is such bullshit. I shouldn't have to torture myself when there's a fucking key next door and a man who has zero plans to use it. I have the sudden urge for him to see me, to take one last look at what he's done.

Scooting off the bed, I yank my trunks up and whip the tweezers at my wall. I'm not going to need them. Rory McDonnell is going to get this thing off me, whether he likes it or not. He's going to look at me, talk to me, and have to deal with me. If it stops him from calculating his next sexual mark, it's the least I can do for humanity. He wanted me. He's going to get me. He can't just throw me away.

CHAPTER 12

I wish the alcohol hadn't worn off as much as it has. A flutter of nerves takes flight in my belly. I'd run back to my room and do a shot for more courage if I hadn't already beaten on Rory's door like a repo man. What am I even worried about?

I can stand his teasing and his riddles. I've tolerated them well enough already. But what if he turns me away? What do I do then?

He wouldn't. Would he?

The door cracks open, revealing him in all his wet, naked glory. His chest is devoid of one tiny silver key. A cloud of steam looms in the air behind him, seeping out of his bathroom. He looks… good wet.

The surprise on his face feels like a small victory, and at the same time, annoys me. Who else did he expect to come calling so late? The towel around his hips is clenched in his grip. As he tucks it in on itself, I find myself licking my lips.

"Charlie… To what do I owe the pleasure?"

Ignoring his fake pleasantries, I charge past him, bumping his shoulder on the way. His cabin is like a portal, sucking me deeper inside as though I'm on autopilot. I have no plan, I realize, other than I wanted him to have to see me.

Stopping at the side of his bed, I stare down at the clean comforter, wondering if he changed his own linens or if his crew is accustomed to cleaning up his sex messes. I resent being a mess that's erased by a trip to the laundry, not that I'd expect anyone to sleep under a pool of my cum.

"Did you enjoy the activities today?" he calls casually.

He's still by the doorway, not stalking me like he did the last time. What's with the small talk? He's never made small talk with me. The threat of being dismissed now, just as easily as his soiled linens, sets in a panic. I hook my thumbs in the waistband of my trunks and drop them to the floor.

"Go get the key," I tell him without turning around.

When I'm met with silence, I climb onto the bed to let him know I have no plans of leaving. He's still in the room. I can feel it from the thickness in the air, but I refuse to look at him the way he refused to look at me all day.

The sound of soft footsteps on the carpeting moving toward the bathroom after a moment allows me to let out a long exhale. It means he's listening. Good. Wiping my sweaty palms on the tops of my thighs, I notice the way I'm trembling already. Glancing up, I catch a nature program playing on his television, baffling me that he was in here watching this rather than seeking me out. I turn around and face the headboard. The thought of watching a documentary about spiders in the jungle isn't the distraction I want for whatever is about to happen next.

I hear him return and ponder the odd curiosity of how his freshly washed skin must feel. I…haven't touched him. He's only touched me. Why do I feel cheated? It's not like I ever sought to touch him.

Leaning forward, I place my hands on the mattress near his pillows so I don't look like a statue. I know the deal. If I ask for something, he'll want something in return, and I'm not playing that game tonight. At least, I don't plan on debating it verbally. If he gets off on getting other people off, he can damn well do it with me instead of some new customer from his club.

Does he have regulars there that he sees? Does he participate in that group flogging night that he mentioned?

I realize he's paused halfway to the bed, but I don't dare look. Good. Maybe I shocked him for once instead of the other way around.

The sound of his towel swishing moves closer. His slender fingers appear at my right, placing the chain with the key on it down on the nightstand. And then…he stands. Silently. Like he's waiting.

I stare at that little silver key, wondering what it means. Of course, it means freedom is mere inches away from me. All I'd have to do is reach out and grab it. I could probably do so quicker than him, but I sense it's another test.

Or perhaps…it's not a test at all. Not the kind I imagined. I think he's…waiting. Waiting to see if I take my chance.

Damn it. Damn it to hell.

My face burns, and I turn my head away to hide the truth on it. I'm not here for a key. Not really. I knew that even before I decided to storm over here. And now…*he* knows it too.

He sucks in a ragged breath that spreads gooseflesh all over my body like wildfire. It's a sound of approval that goes right to my nuts. I'm in awe of just how much I've yearned for that approval.

"Shirt off," he whispers. "You're covered in sand."

I blink through a wave of embarrassment for being scolded. A splash of misery for disappointing him in even the most trivial way. Sitting up, I reach for the hem of my tank top and start drawing it over my head. Fingers brush the back of my neck, making me shiver, and he helps me tug it over my head.

I watch it fall to the floor at his bare feet. When the bottom of his towel sways, I lean forward and plant my hands back on the mattress in an effort to look away. The soft sound of it dropping to the floor heightens my building arousal and the fear that I seem to get off on. Is he naked? Fully naked?

He just got out of the shower. Why would he put his Speedo back on? Of course, he's probably naked.

"Grab the lube for me, handsome, will you?" he croons and walks off toward the door.

I cringe at the order, but reach for it even as I do. Pulling the drawer open, I'm well aware of the key sitting on the surface of the nightstand just above my hand. It's like it's taunting me, telling me I don't have to do this…whatever *this* is. It's no longer a symbol of freedom, but rather an icon denoting two paths—one where I grab it and walk out of here. Another, where I ignore it and free-fall into the spell Rory casts over me, beckoning me to be '*brave*' and try new things.

The lights dim, calming my trepidation and spiking my anticipation. It's beginning—everything I don't know that I'm asking for.

The padding sound of his footsteps on the carpeting returns. A hand slides down my forearm and covers the bottle in mine. Lips dust feather light against my shoulder as he pulls it from my grip.

"Thank you," he whispers.

A hand trails down my spine and circles over the small of my back. I'm suddenly buzzed again, as though his touch is the equivalent of drinking four beers.

"You keep surprising me, Charlie. I'm so proud of you."

Proud of me? For what? Through my wondering, I feel myself preening over that odd bit of praise. My dick hums in approval.

The sound of the lube cap flicking open interrupts my latest self-discovery. I try to breathe evenly so he won't know just how much I'm reacting to this peculiar dance. His palm slides across the top of my ass and grips my hip. He uses me to leverage himself onto the bed, treating my body as a handle. It's something I imagine familiar lovers do or disrespectful clients of sex workers. I'm oddly aroused by either similarity, both being used by and being familiar to him.

His other palm runs over my taint and then my balls until he reaches the cable of the cage. I wince at the soreness there from all my movements today during the volleyball match when his lubed fingers connect.

"Aw, baby…didn't you lube this up before the match?"

Baby… I trip over that word for a moment, and its effect on me. I've never cared for it and usually roll my eyes when I hear it in movies. Perhaps it's that I finally have his concern and undivided attention that's the real allure.

"No," I mumble.

"Promise me, if you plan to keep wearing it, that you'll take better care of yourself."

That makes it sound like I have the option. I don't understand. Is it his way of reminding me that the key is readily available within my reach? Does he not want me to wear it any longer? I mean, not that I planned to, but suddenly, it seems strange to imagine going back to life without it on. I've grown so…used to it.

He doesn't press me for an answer, continuing to massage the tender skin around my sac. It's pleasant just like the other times, but there's an eagerness building inside of me. His favorite word, '*greedy*,' comes to mind, considering I just came last night. It feels like we're living on borrowed time, though, with the cruise ending tomorrow. After that, all this chaos stops. I have to go back to my normal life without cock cages and strange compliments.

His hand moves to the cage. A greasy fingertip surprises me, swiping down the slit in my cock. The bigger surprise is the feel of teeth on my right ass cheek. It was just a nibble, nothing painful, but unexpected. My cock twitches inside the cage. He must have noticed because he makes that satisfied hum and moves to my other cheek, treating it to the same biting action. Will I have teeth marks when he's done? Picturing it, I warm from head to toe.

His whiskers brush across my ass, bringing the flesh to life. Lips touch down on my hole and stay, holding a kiss there.

I shudder and blow out a breath, trying not to tremble at the reverence of the act. My thighs inch further apart. It's a covert way of giving my thanks. When he gives a hum of approval, I'm grateful he can't see me blush.

His mouth leaves, and I'm left in the darkness with only the low hum of the television, wondering what his next move is. Is it just the unknown that thrills me? Rory's not an unknown. I've messed around with him more times than I have with anyone besides my old college fuck buddy. Will I grow unenthralled once he's run through all his moves like I did with that college tryst?

"Sorry. It's time for your favorite part," he warns just before I hear the squelch of the lube bottle.

A cool dribble hits the top of my seam and runs downward. I stiffen, still not used to having lube there, but then his fingers swirl through my crease just like they did last night. A sound of relief floods out of me from that light contact. I can't believe I was actually hoping he'd give me a repeat of the treatment he did last night. A repeat! Listen to me!

It has to be the curiosity of coming while in the cage. Will I be able to feel like that again, or was last night just a one-off?

"This was such a nice surprise," he murmurs, circling my rim. And then he taps the center with his fingertip. "Such…" My hole spasms against the contact, and he continues, "a lovely…" I spasm in response again. "Surprise."

Fucking hell. He's playing me like an instrument, and my body is singing on command. The pressure in my balls and cock has reached the point of discomfort again, even after that maddening release yesterday. *Want* is quickly becoming *need*. He'd better do more than tap soon, so I don't resort to begging again.

"Are you ready, Charlie?" he whispers, holding the tip of his finger against my heat.

My hole is practically grabbing at him, and he's asking me that? I let out a frustrated scoff, hoping he doesn't expect an actual reply. I want to get back to climbing toward an orgasm, not redirecting toward sexual frustration.

"Uhn!" He forces the noise out of my mouth by slipping his finger inside to the second knuckle without further preamble.

The satisfied sigh I let out as I absorb the sensation of fulfillment should embarrass me, but I don't let it. I deserve this. I think I earned it well enough.

He starts working his finger in slow thrusts, pausing to glide over my prostate every few insertions. It's even more wonderful than last night, now that it's not my first rodeo. Except, the longer it goes on, the more it becomes not wonderful enough.

A thick, satisfied sound purrs behind me. "Mmm."

I freeze as the back of one of my thighs slams into the front of one of his. How long have I been ramming my ass back onto his finger? When did he stop doing all the work? Oh, God.

"No. Don't stop. I was quite enjoying that."

I want to oblige, but I can't bring myself to move. So, I just stay poised, his finger jammed deep in my ass. Biting my lip, I send up a silent plea that he'll take pity on me. My cock is leaking, so it gives me hope I won't have to suffer much longer.

Sighing, he retracts his finger, breaking a piece of my heart. Shit. I fucked this up.

"Greedy and yet still so shy." I feel his middle finger line up next to his index finger at my rim, then, lighting me up with relief. "It's all right, Charlie. It's what attracted me to you in the first place."

He thought I was shy? Maybe I just gave off a normal reaction to being handed a card to a private sex club. As I hold my breath and wait for those two fingers to deliver, however, the *'attracted'* part tumbles around in my brain. I stow it on a secret shelf in my mind next to the word *'handsome'* like a trophy. A rush of preening trickles across my skin.

There's pressure, but my body gives way easily. It knows it has a welcome visitor and acts like a practiced host now. My moan falls freely from my lips this time. I'm over any shame when I adjust to the fullness inside me. It's like a missing piece has been put into place, making me more whole.

"And this ass," he murmurs, rubbing his other palm over one of my cheeks and giving it a squeeze. "I knew it would be just as perfect as that cock of yours."

I groan, low and long, at the praise. I can't help it, combined with the exquisite fullness and zings to my gland. It's amping me up, pumping blood to where I need it.

It goes on and on; the mattress jiggling beneath us with each thrust of his fingers. The nature documentary murmurs in the background. It's just me, Rory, the darkness, and those two bold fingers. We're a dirty secret, rocking in time with the ship while everyone else is sleeping.

The pressure of the cable grows firmer against my swollen sac. My cock reached the capacity of the cage five long minutes ago. Why haven't I come yet?

My moans have morphed into grunts now. I wait, but nothing happens. There's just the sensation of my release being blocked and…not quite there. If he could just…graze my gland a little better. More like he did yesterday. Maybe I could…

Shit. *Am I* being greedy? Was this too much to ask after that release yesterday?

I swear, though, it feels like Rory isn't using the same technique. He's only tapping my bundle of nerves every three or four strokes now. Half the time, his fingertips glide around the outside of it. If I didn't know better, I'd say he's either distracted or… Is he half-assing it on purpose to prolong things?

"P-please," I stammer.

"What?"

Fuck. Why did he remove his fingers? That's not what I meant.

Panting, I angle my head back and catch sight of his naked hip shadowed by the glow from the TV behind him. Dropping my head, I redirect my eyes back to the mattress, trying to blot out the reminder that he's completely naked.

"Do something."

His hands take two handfuls of my ass. They knead the meat there as though my flesh is dough, and he purrs again.

"Tell me what you need, handsome."

When his thumb traces up my seam, I shiver. My hole clenches between my squished cheeks, angry that it's being ignored.

"Fuck," I whisper, gritting my teeth at the fact he's somehow managed to bring me to the point of begging again. "Fuck," I repeat, but then the simple answer to my problems tumbles from my lips when I add, "*me.*"

"Mm. Gladly," he croons, leaning over me, covering my back with his chest.

His hands alight on the mattress right next to mine. I can smell his spicy soap scent as his hair tickles the back of my shoulders when he places a kiss at the base of my neck.

"How?" he asks, moving his mouth to the side of my neck for another kiss. "With my tongue?" Grazing the back of my neck with his open mouth, he moves to the other side, trailing his lips up to behind my ear. If I don't sound like I'm winded from the thrill, it's a miracle.

"With my fingers?" he suggests, nipping at my earlobe.

At that same moment, something hot and solid presses between my ass cheeks. My eyes flare open to the blue glow from the TV on the pillows. I can feel his hip bones press into my cheeks. I can feel the veins in his cock nestle right up against my seam.

God, he's so hard. Hard for *me.*

A shaky whimper escapes me, a needy, wanton, and possibly slightly terrified sound. But I don't move. As far as my pucker is concerned, his cock is a magnet. It tries to take hold, giving his silky flesh a little kiss as I spasm and whimper again.

Lowering his head, he rests his mouth on my shoulder. I feel a smile press to my skin.

"Mm," he hums, giving his hips a little nudge. "Or, yes…there is *that*," he says, as though he's agreeing with something I said.

Rising, his cock slides between my sticky cheeks and then he pulls away. What does that mean?

His hands go to my hips and glide over my ass soothingly. "Turn around for me."

Turn around? If I turn around, I'll…have to look at him. I'll *see* him.

"I need your help with something," he amends, as though he senses my stage fright.

The human instinct that makes a person answer a call for assistance has me rising slowly to my knees. I don't turn around, though, only glance over my shoulder. His hand grabs one of mine. I look down when I feel him place the bottle of lube into my palm.

He shifts to the side at the same time he urges me by the shoulder. I angle around slowly, glancing down at his cock. It's the first time I've seen it, and it steals my breath. Guiding my waist, he helps me face him. I move, dumbstruck like a rag doll, gaping at his erection and the way it's pointing right at me.

I sneak glimpses of his shadowed face and feel mine burn. It's so…personal, and I hate myself for my fear of seeing my partner. Millions of people in the world look at each other when they're intimate. Why can't I? I can hear all my brothers' teasing about how I've never once brought a girl home. I can hear all their detailed comments about the women they've been with over the years, and how those conversations about brotherly rites of passage always left me feeling like a fraud among them. What would they say if they ever found out what I do in the dark?

Guiding my other hand, he cups it around the underside of his cock, pulling a gasp from me. He's warm and heavy against my palm, and I like the way he feels. Like feeling him against my skin. Like holding him in my grip as though he's trusting me with this part of himself.

He flicks the lid of the lube open, moves my other hand, and squeezes it, making the liquid spill out onto him.

My lungs heave, feeling the liquid dribble around him and into my palm. I blink, mesmerized by the sight of him in my hand.

"Get me good and ready, Charlie." He takes the bottle from me, tosses it aside, and circles the wrist of my other hand, urging it to turn. "I'd never forgive myself if I hurt you."

Right…because…because I just begged him to fuck me. I just asked him to put *this* inside me. I swallow, watching my hand as I twist it around his length, coating him. His breathing sounds like it's difficult for him to control as I slowly work the lube over him, filling me with a flutter of delight. He *likes* my touch.

Drawing my hand away, he takes his other one and smears it over my palm, transferring the excess liquid onto his own. I blink dumbly, even though I have an idea of why he did it.

I hover there, immobile, just blinking down between us. His cock glistening under the glow of the TV, mine shimmering in its cage.

"I'm ready," he whispers, brushing the edge of my jaw with his thumb.

The adoring touch gives me a start. I spin back around and plant my hands on the mattress like a small animal that's been spooked back into its burrow. I'm safe like this, in this position. Where I can experience all the pleasure he possesses without having to face him. Without him seeing the pleasure on my face.

My heart thumps as the seconds tick by. Do I really want this? What if I can't handle it and have to ask him to stop? Why do I care about letting him down? Why do I not want to let myself down about something I've never wanted before?

A hand rests on my hip, and he leans forward, reconnecting us. As soon as I feel his slick heat pressed against me again, I know my answer. I want it. I want it badly. Or at least want to try.

His lubed finger traces a circle over that sensitive spot above my tailbone, making me shudder. "I'm bigger than my fingers," he warns gently, rocking so that his tip glances back and forth over my hole. "Are you sure you can take me?"

It sounds like a dare, spiking a flicker of anger in me. My eyes were about to cross at the maddening sensation of the bulbous cockhead grazing my pucker, but the panic of him possibly denying me cripples the thrill. I press back sharply, determined.

Grunting, my ring stretches. It's a good stretch for a moment, a promise of soon being filled, until it isn't. The good stretch turns into a burn, and I let out a little cry, terrified I won't be able to do it. But then the pressure gives way and there's a popping sensation as his cockhead slides through my ring of muscles.

I sputter, frozen, jaw hanging wide open. Speared by just that meaty tip, I shudder at the sensation of hot flesh inside me. A cock. For the first time. It's a thick intrusion, filling me more than his fingers ever did. There's a soreness all the way around my ring, telling me I'm probably at capacity for how far I can stretch, but just the knowledge of that inch of *him* inside *me* sends a flutter through my belly that seeps into my groin.

"Mm," he groans, tracing his palm over my lower back and running another up and down the outside of my thigh. "That's a good start, handsome."

Two of his fingers slide down to the place where he's entered me and trace my stretched ring delicately, easing the burn. He's touched me there before, but feeling him touch me while I'm expanded around him is… God, I don't know. Humiliating? Erotic as all fuck?

I groan, my head falling. Shivers trickle down my legs, and my hole relaxes. The second it does, I feel him slip further inside, which has my sounds deepening.

He groans with me, a low, satisfied sound that has me preening with vibrations. His index finger returns to the small of my back, drawing little circles over that spot that makes my toes curl. I rock backward without even thinking, too lulled by that delicious erogenous zone he's discovered.

The rim of his cockhead slips over my gland, and I convulse. I'm sucking in air now, like I'm breathing through a straw. The pressure is immense. It's like he's taken over my body, owning it. I'm no longer me. I'm Rory's cock.

Inhaling, he leans over me, dropping his chest to my back and caging his arms around mine. "I'm so proud of you," he whispers, sounding pained as his lips brush my hairline.

I keen a peculiar noise, unable to speak. His heat and weight comfort me, relaxing the last round of my muscle's tension. Slowly, he nudges the rest of his way in. His hips press tight against my ass. The soft tuft at his groin is brushing against my hole. He's deep. So deep. He's…all mine. Every inch.

I did it.

My channel clenches around him, but with how full I am, it's more like a quiver. He grunts behind my ear. The feral sound delights my senses, lighting up every cell in my body. I moan around another filthy, involuntary hug of his cock like my body is trying to pull him deeper. He can't go deeper. I don't think I have any room to spare. If I had a contents label, it would read *100% Rory.*

Sucking in a breath, he presses his lips to my neck, and palms my ass cheek, giving it a squeeze. "You've got me. All of me," he rasps. "Do you feel it?"

I gasp, but he stays silent. I squirm against him, trying to tell him there's no way I can form words to reply even if I wanted to. So, I just moan another desperate sound. The pressure is such a precarious sensation, and yet, I feel oddly comforted beyond thought. It's as though giving myself over so completely has freed me from my earthly troubles and cares.

"No one else has been here…have they?" he asks, circling his palm over my ass cheek.

I want to pretend I don't know what he means. Why does it matter? Why did he need to ask? And how can he tell? Am I…bad at this, even though we've just started?

"Oh, Charlie," he whispers, nuzzling my cheek as my face burns. I don't want him to know it's burning because I don't mind that it's him.

Kissing the back of my jaw, he rocks us forward with a little nudge. His hand trails underneath me. It slides up my abdomen, then to my stomach, and presses there.

"I knew this ass was made for me," he whispers, sounding drunk. "Thank you for giving it to me." Another kiss, and then he sighs. "We're going to enjoy it together now."

He says the most perverse and possessive things that leave my head spinning. I was…*made for him?* No one's made for any-one, but my channel seems to think otherwise, hugging him again as my cock pushes at my cage.

Righting himself, he gets to his knees. I'm left exposed without his chest covering me, poised here like a statue, stuffed full of Rory. Gripping my hips, he eases back, dragging his cockhead over my gland. There's a strange suction as he draws himself out to just before his tip. I don't like the wake of emptiness it leaves behind. My vocal cords let him know. He rubs the small of my back like he understands and then eases back in. A balloon of pleasure mushrooms deep in my abdomen, making my balls sing. He does it again, and the pleasure amplifies through every fiber of my being.

My elbows give out. I drop my forehead to my forearms, stunned to helplessness by the sensations. Empty. Full. Loss. Saved.

Over and over, he takes and gives. I'm a wound-up coil of need, my cock dripping onto the comforter. He's going to get me there. I can just tell.

"Charlie," he whispers, his hips kicking up their pace. "Oh, Charlie."

Fuck. It's so good. Everything. Even my name on his lips, no matter how unnecessary. How is it this good?

The first slap of his hips against my ass has me belting out a cry. At least, I thought it was a cry. It's not until that spanking sensation jostles me several times with bolts of pleasure that I hear myself with more clarity.

"Rory! Rory…"

Oh, God. How many times have I called out his name? I chomp down on my bottom lip and whimper. This is madness. Can too much pleasure consume a person? I want it to end, and yet it seems like it would be a fool's request to wish this kind of experience to cease prematurely.

"Come on, Charlie. You can do it." Rory's palm runs up my spine and then zigzags back down as though he wants to touch as much of me as he can. His fingertips leave tingling behind as they go. Does everything about him cast a spell?

It must because his next words have me granting his request on command. "Come for me, Charlie. Let me feel you come on my cock."

That dam of pressure behind the cable bursts, lofting me to a height I've never known. The world goes black. My head, light. There is nothing but me, Rory, and a wave of euphoria that crashes over me. The waves keep coming. Just when I think it can't go on any longer, he makes a long guttural sound and pulses inside me. My eyes flare open, but all I see are spots. It's an odd sensation of being filled with heat, but then my channel clenches around him in time with his pulses. While it's so foreign, there's something about it that makes perfect sense. We've become our own nature program—my body drawing from him in time with our need. I don't have to worry about either liking or hating him. About him knowing my secrets or my kinks. About the world or anyone knowing what we're doing. About judgment or insecurity. It's just perfection. Two bodies that are in complete harmony. His growls and moans rain down on me as I siphon his release. Once again, I'm greedy, just like he said. I surrender to it, collapsing back down onto my arms, riding through the unavoidable reaction.

When my breathing finally slows, and I manage to open my eyes, it's like being born. I'm warm and so sated; it should be a new definition of serenity.

The touch of lips to the back of my shoulder gives me pause. I'm on my side. Rory is behind me. That warmth I feel is coming from his chest pressed to my back and his arms wrapped around me. How long have we been lying here like this?

One of his hands runs down my side and stops on my hip. I can feel his spent cock pressed against the back of my thigh. Glancing down, I find a pool of my release in front of me. Hell, how did I come so much again?

"Are you all right?" he asks.

I can't believe he's asking me that, like I'm some kind of virgin. Worse yet, I can't believe the concern fills me with even more warmth. I have no idea if I'm all right. How can I be? I just let Rory McDonnell fuck me and now he's spooning me while I light up over his words of aftercare.

I nod once and let out a grunt, trying to figure out how I can disentangle myself. What happens now? Surely, he'll get up and make some snarky remark soon. Thank goodness this cruise is over tomorrow. I can go back to Portland and bury myself in my routine without having to interact with him again. We won't ever have to talk about this. Our strange association outside of work is done.

His palm slides to my stomach, though. Whiskers nuzzle my neck, and his thumb rubs back and forth over my abs.

"Do you have any idea how happy you've made me?"

I feel that intimate whisper all the way to the deepest part of my tender channel. Is he doling out lip service as a consolation prize for his victory over me falling for his charms? No one can mean the things this guy says, even if they are good for my ego.

"I dreamt about you being in my bed so many times," he murmurs, giving me a squeeze and cuddling closer. He...what?

"Wait until you see the one at my house," he continues. "You'll never want to leave it."

His house? Does he think I'm going to come over for a repeat...at *his house?* How...how would that work if I even wanted to? I can't believe I did this once, and he's talking like he has me in the bag.

Oh God, he's kissing my neck again. My heart thumps thick in my throat. This is... It's bad.

I can't become some secret plaything of the damn CEO. Tensing, I suck in a breath and push myself up, but I don't get far.

"Hey, hang on. We made quite the mess," he chuckles.

The mattress shifts, and I see my opening when he gets up. Swinging my legs over the side of the bed, I'm poised to get up and snag my trunks. Instead, I freeze and clench my asscheeks together.

He's right. We *did* make a mess. His release dribbles out
of me.

Oh, fuck. I'm leaking on his bed a foot away from where I just
left a small lake.

Rory turns back to me with his towel in his hand. There's a
strange smile on his face. It's not the mischievous ones I've seen
before. This one looks almost adoring. It must be how self-conscious I feel at the moment. He drops to a knee in front of me like
he's going to clean me up the way he did the other day.

How much clean-up is he planning? My ass too? And
then what?

First, all that crazy shit he said. Then, he insinuated that I could
come to his house. What is happening? I don't want to find out. I
have to get out of here.

Springing up, I sidestep past him, avoiding eye contact. Bending down, I snag up my shorts, cringing when something warm
dribbles down the inside of my thigh. I stuff my feet into the
leg openings of my damp trunks, hopping toward the door with
each step.

"Hey, hold on. Don't you want to—"

"I'm good," I cut him off. "I'll…shower in my room. Goodnight."

I'm almost in the clear, mere feet from the door. He must think
I'm so disgusting, sliding my trunks up my legs with an ass full of
cum dripping from me and my cock covered in my release. I don't
give a fuck, though. I'm in survival mode.

"Charlie, wait."

I freeze. Why do I freeze? The door handle is right there. How
come I stop every time he calls my name?

I feel a hand at my waist. Naturally, I turn like a freaking pup-
pet, helpless to his touch.

"I think you forgot something."

Raising my gaze, I don't connect with his. I stop on the key
dangling from the chain in his grasp.

Holy shit. I still have the cage on. The *locked* cage. The freaking reason I told myself I came in here in the first place. If it were
possible to melt into a puddle of lava on the floor rright now, I'd
do so.

Dropping to his knees, he waits. Once again, I strip for a man
I never thought I'd strip for, lowering my trunks to just below my
cock. He's still naked. The glow from the TV painting enough light
on him that the definition of his body looks like a work of art right
now. The position is all too similar to our first interaction in his
club, making my knees weak.

I'm positive I have congealed cum clinging to my cage, but he makes no protests, gently gripping my cage. It shifts, and I feel the lock give way when he turns the key. The cable loosens, and he slips it over my sac, freeing me.

It's nothing at all what I imagined it would feel like. I feel light as air, so light it's like my cock and balls are missing even though I can see they're still attached to me. I'm free. Finally free, but it feels like I've lost something.

Glancing up at me, he's silent. I wait. I don't know if I'm expecting him to speak. He always seems to be two steps ahead of me, and so self-assured, I just assumed he'd have something to say. Maybe I wait because I want him to say something, but he doesn't. I certainly have no idea what to say. And I'm pretty sure it has everything to do with that look of hope in his eyes.

Is he waiting for me to ask him to put it back on? For a second, I consider it.

And then…I regain my fucking senses. What the actual fuck am I thinking? Why would I want it back on when my life's goal since the second he slapped it on me was to get it off?

Turning without a word, I yank my trunks up and wrench the door open. I breeze down the corridor in swift strides, my spent cock wagging back and forth in freedom. I'm free, I remind myself as I open the door to my cabin. As a twinge of emptiness washes over me, I remind myself again—I'm free.

CHAPTER 13

I curse at the fancy sports car parked on the street way too close to the entrance of my driveway. They mustn't value it enough if they'd risk it getting sideswiped by parking like an idiot. Parking my SUV, I let out a sigh. I never used to have anything against Mondays. I've never understood people who do. My ass, however, feels like it's dragging from the grind of work for the third in a row now. It's been two weeks since I've been back from the most fucked-up cruise to ever cruise. I was supposed to be happy to return to my routine, but work has lost its luster.

Making my way to my front door, I grind my teeth, knowing that's not exactly true. Work is fine. I'm just…distracted. If I could stop thinking about a certain CEO and the cruise activities that I got up to with said CEO, everything might feel more like it's gone back to normal. I don't want to quit. Quitting won't change what happened. Why should I quit? I kick ass at my job. I don't have to see or talk to him. His name is on several mass emails now and then, but it always has been. It doesn't matter that I now know what the face of that name looks like or…the rest of him. And what the rest of him…feels like.

"For fuck's sake, Charlie," I grumble to myself, unlocking my house.

Maybe it's because I haven't forgotten that little tease he dropped about me getting the promotion. Was there even a fucking promotion? If so, I've not heard a word about it. Certainly nothing from one *Riordan* McDonnell. The bastard.

It was all bullshit. Wasn't it? He toyed with me to get me to let him fuck me, and it worked.

Growling, I curse under my breath when the lock sticks. He's still so much in my head that I can't even focus enough to unlock my fucking door.

Mostly, I hate the complete and utter mush that has become my brain for thinking shit like that. I would never let someone fuck me just to get a promotion, so I know that's my pride talking. I… did what I did because…well, because I couldn't help myself.

Whatever. I tried something new. That's human growth. Right? It's supposed to be good for people. Even people who don't need to change.

I just…don't like the idea of being…forgotten. Snorting, I shake my head and turn the key the right way, like a sane person this time, unlocking my door. Why the fuck do I care if Rory McDonnell forgot about me? Part of me can't believe that he would, though. After all the things he said.

And that's the other thing that doesn't make any sense. The more I go over everything in my head, the more I can't sell myself on the idea I was just a game to him. Who puts as much thought into everything he said and did just to have a one- or two-night stand with someone?

That combination—the one he gave me for the first lock on the cage—I think it means something. I mean… to me it does at least.

Going through my calendar last week, I got distracted—imagine that—and rehashed a timeline of interacting with a certain someone. *1-0-2-5*. That was the combination he gave me. *1-0-2-5*—October twenty-fifth. The date of the Seattle convention I met him at last year. Is it a coincidence? How can it be?

But what does it mean if it's not? What does it matter? It would only matter if I *wanted* it to mean something, which I don't. Because I'm over the entire ordeal.

A knock at the door has me nearly jumping out of my skin. If it's one of my freaking brothers right now, I don't have the patience to deal with them. I love them in my own way, but it's like listening to someone speak a foreign language whenever we talk. Wives, girlfriends, kids, Little League games, home repairs. There's never talk about cock or just hiring a contractor to do home repairs right because some of us weren't born with brain cells that give a shit about learning home remodeling. Honestly, I think I'd die if any of my brothers were into guys and tried talking to me about men. Right. I need to quit my bitching. Everything's fine being Greek between us.

"Hey, Mr. North!" my mailman greets me when I answer the door. Thank fuck, it's just him. "I've got one that needs a signature today."

I take the stiff cardboard mailer from him and close the door. Inspecting the label, I go as rigid as the envelope. The addressee reads, *Riordan McDonnell*. I know for a fact the return address under his name isn't the address to headquarters. It's from an address in the Northwest Heights area of Portland.

He said his home was in Northwest Heights, didn't he? He sent this with his home address as the return label? Why would he do that?

My throat goes thick at the possibility he wants me to know where he lives. Why the fuck would I want to know where he lives?

Making my way to my kitchen island, I tear open the seal, ignoring the way my hand trembles. Maybe it's photos, and he's going to blackmail me over our...our...whatever the hell it was.

He's a billionaire, Charlie. Why the fuck would he blackmail you? And besides, it's lumpy. It can't be just photos.

Oh my God. Is it another sex device?

I give myself a mental slap when my cock twitches at the thought. I still don't understand why my dick has felt like it's been tranquilized since returning, unless I think about you-know-who. Pinching my eyes shut, I shake my head over how my trip to a club over the weekend signified that aggravating factoid. I was horny—horny from thinking about you-know-who. Or...what I did with you-know-who. At least, that's what I told myself when I entered that dark club in Seattle on Saturday night. No fucking way was I chancing going to one in Portland and running into him. Not that he probably goes to gay clubs in Portland—he fucking has his own private one. Why would he need to?

I had a shot or three for courage and danced. It didn't take long to feel a willing body grinding up against mine once I hit the dance floor. It took about the same amount of time to make it to my SUV with the guy, and then...then it took way too fucking long to realize my cock wasn't going to work. Because...because he didn't sound like Rory. Didn't smell like Rory. Didn't feel like Rory. And maybe even because I didn't...because my junk wasn't locked up...locked up by Rory.

I *will* get over this...

I will.

Just as soon as I see what's in this fucking envelope.

Reaching inside, nothing bites me. I pull out a packet of papers stapled together. My eyes scan over the works of a letterhead. It's professional. It's Amor's logo. Rory's signature is at the bottom. I read and then reread again. And again.

It's…the promotion. I got the promotion.

I fan through the packet, catching a statement of work outlining the new position. There's a benefits package that makes my eyes nearly boggle out of their sockets, and onboarding forms for me to sign if I choose to accept.

When I find myself scouring the fine print to see if there are punishments for violations, I give myself a mental slap over the flicker of disappointment that trickles through me when I find none. It looks legit. Professional. Entirely work-related.

Glancing at the mailer, I notice it's still bowed open. Tipping it upside down, a key fob falls out onto my countertop. I blink at the Porsche logo on it. A Porsche… He's giving me a Porsche as a work car?

Picking it up, I click the lock button and hear a faint chirp outside. I walk to the door like a zombie, holding the fob out as though it's a flashlight helping me see in the darkness. Stepping out onto my porch, I click the button again and watch as the lights on a brand-new Porsche flash near the end of my driveway—the car I nearly sideswiped on my way in.

He delivered a Porsche to my house. Was he here, or did he pay someone to drop it off? It shouldn't give me a dangerous thrill to think he might have been here. He's a billionaire—why would he bother dropping off cars to his employees when he can pay someone? And, of course, he can find my address if he wants. I work for his company. All my information is on file with the HR department.

My shaky legs take me across my lawn to the curb. I should probably be feeling something, but my emotional circuit is so con-fused, I don't know what to feel. Excitement that I got a promo-tion? Excitement that Rory kept his word—that his promise wasn't bullshit? Aroused by the license plate that reads, *RC 1025*? RC… Rory and…Charlie? No. Another coincidence. Right? He wouldn't be so bonkers, he'd put that on there. Would he?

Unless…

For fuck's sake. What is wrong with me? He's corrupted my brain as much as his, if I'm contemplating it. *Rory's…cock?*

Maybe I just have some employee number I don't even know about, and it just happens to be the date I met him at that conven-tion last year. Yeah. That's totally more plausible.

Opening the passenger door, my breath catches at the sheer beauty of the custom leather interior. There's a cell phone with a little red bow on it sitting on the seat. I tremble, reaching to open the notecard attached to it.

Our new CEO of Marketing should have a comfortable ride. Hope you like the color as much as I do.

The car is blue. I can't help but notice it looks like a custom paint job. I've not seen this color on a car. It almost matches the color of my eyes...

Tapping the phone, I don't know what I expect to find on the home screen. A love letter? Again...what the fuck is wrong with me? There's nothing but a generic home screen, which brings me both relief and disappointment. Clicking on the contacts, I still at the sight of three entries. *HQ. HR.* And...*Rory.*

If I fucking accidentally dial him right now and have to talk to him, I'll never forgive myself. Carefully, I click on his screen name, and it brings up his details. I need to know. I just have to. There are three entries in his contact profile. His work landline. His work cell phone. And a third—*Rory Personal Cell.*

He gave me his number. I now have his number. After a rush of shivers fans over my body from head to toe, I suck in a breath. And then...I slam the car door shut and lock it.

It's bait. I fucking know it is. I'm a mouse and he's dangling cheese in front of me, waiting to see if I'll bite.

I won't.

I'll take the job and keep the fucking car. I earned the job, at least. But I won't bite. I'm no fucking mouse.

CHAPTER 14

Two weeks later

He didn't look at me. Not once.

I knew sooner or later I'd have to end up in some kind of meeting with him at headquarters if I took this promotion. I'm not an idiot. And, yes, I knew he'd have to act professionally, the way he did during that welcome dinner on the cruise. He did just that at the quarterly meeting I attended yesterday at HQ. Before the business side of the meeting, he announced my promotion and introduced me to the room. That was the closest I came to being acknowledged by him, though. Each time I made eye contact, he looked away. Trying to catch his attention was like trying to spear a gnat with a needle, I swear.

And those emails over the last two weeks since I took the promotion... Those fucking replies to my emails—could they be any vaguer? He either tells me *Good job, Keep up the great work,* or sends some sanitized response with contacts I can try to tap into for new markets. It's so…condescending. Helpful and clearly work-related, but…condescending. I'm sure anyone who reads the emails would think nothing of them. But if he said them to me in person, I bet he'd have that coy little smirk on his face, and his voice would be dripping with that obnoxious wisdom he seems to possess. Wisdom of dark secrets that people like me don't know.

Okay, I know that sounds totally ridiculous. But that's kind of the point—he's turned me into a ridiculous person. Gripping the steering wheel, I grit my teeth as I stare at the lit pathway to the front door of his house. I was headed to meet a *Grindr* hook-up. I *was*, but I ended up here instead. Somehow, a right became a left and then another right, and then I was…here.

He's in there. Right now. I can tell. His car is in his driveway, and there are a few lights on inside, but that's not how I know. I can sense his presence. It's the fucking reason I'm sitting in his driveway like a damn super fan.

It doesn't matter what I do or who I try to do it with. No amount of self-pleasure tactics, sex toys, or hook-ups is going to work. I know because I've tried it all over the past month since the cruise. The only thing that comes close to working is when I think about *him*. *Me*…with *him*. Me with him and… my cage. His…*gift.*

I even fucking bought another one, but I don't like it. It doesn't fit the same. It doesn't feel the same. It's not…his. And this isn't a conversation I'm going to have at work, over a phone call, or via text message. If he didn't want me to have his home address, he shouldn't have put it on my promotion packet.

Shoving out of the car, I make my way past the lights lining his sidewalk toward an ominous black door illuminated under a covered porch. The white stucco contemporary-style house is impressive, yet I'm surprised it's not larger and more elaborate, considering his wealth. He could certainly afford a mansion if he wanted. A set of stacked windows affords the only glimpse of the interior. The other windows are narrow and rectangular, close to the soffit. It's the perfect architecture for a man who needs privacy. What the hell does he get up to here, I wonder.

Squaring my shoulders, I step onto the porch and knock, determined. Desperate. Once again, miserable. My heart hammers when the latch disengages. The black door opens, silhouetting Rory in a warm glow of light from deeper inside the house.

He's in worn jeans, slung low on his hips. The sleeves of his white Henley are shoved up to his elbows, a hint of chest hair peeking out behind the three undone buttons between his clavicles. The sight of his bare feet makes me feel like I'm intruding on something personal for some reason. Well, of course I am. This is his home, but I don't care. I need answers.

"Charlie…is everything all right?"

I resent the instant assumption that I'm only here because something is wrong and not because he waved a covert invitation in my face by sending me his home address. Brushing past him, I step inside, ignoring how it looks like I invited myself in. His spicy scent hits me like a brick wall. It's everywhere. I've just entered the honey pot of Rory's aroma. This is terrible. How am I going to be able to think with his smell all around me?

"No, as a matter of fact," I huff, taking in the open floor plan.

There's a kitchen off to my right, through an archway. The scent of grilled food tickles my nose. I don't know if I'm surprised he cooks for himself or not surprised at all, considering he seems to be a man of particular taste.

The walnut flooring extends across a wide hallway in front of me, all the way through the living room to a wall of floor-to-ceiling windows. While his house appears to be a modern fortress from the outside, his view to the rear is open, overlooking Mt. Hood. As my pulse flickers with adrenaline, I scan my surroundings for signs of anything risqué, or possibly an indicator that he has company. All I see is a serene home with minimalist paintings on the walls and a few abstract sculptures on the floor lining the hallway.

"What's going on?"

The door clicks shut behind me, ratcheting up my heart rate. Anyone else would think what I'm about to say is absurd. I'm sure of it. But this is Rory. He's the one who got me into this mess.

I try to control my breathing, feeling him approach. I don't need him to be closer to say what I'm going to say. It's a greedy bit of narcissism, why I wait—the strange addiction that brought me to his doorstep tonight. I can feel my blood growing warmer the closer he gets, feel my flesh going taut.

Snap out of it, Charlie. That's why you're here—to figure out how to get rid of those reactions, not to fall prey to more of them.

"What did you do to me?" The hoarse demand falls from my lips.

Judging by his silence, he either didn't hear me, he's waiting for me to elaborate, or he knows exactly what I mean. Pinching my eyes closed, I take a breath through my mouth so I don't have to get another hit of his intoxicating scent.

"I can't...*function*...like I used to."

The floor creaks, making me happy there's at least one thing that's imperfect about him or his life and possessions. "Function how?"

He's close. His body heat is warm on my skin, making me want to be reached out to and touched. I swallow against the thickness in my throat.

"Nothing...works. I...I can barely get off anymore unless...unless..." Fuck that. I'm not going there—not giving him the satisfaction. "And when I do, it's...disappointing."

"You're going through a dry spell and assume our time together is to blame?"

This bastard. Spinning around, I level my gaze on him but get no satisfaction. He looks positively curious, invested. I don't detect a trace of smugness in his expression.

"I don't know what's to blame. I just know that I used to feel good, and now I don't. I used to have a sex life where I didn't think about having a cage on my cock or…" I refuse to say the words, '*your cock in my ass*,' and hope he can't read between the lines.

Why does he look surprised? There's something else there, too, though. I think it's empathy. I don't want empathy. I want…

God, I can't look at him any longer. Lowering my gaze, I search for a way to sum up my new predicament. "You…you fucking broke me."

I see his feet inch forward. A thumb grazes my jaw, sending a shiver down my spine. "What do you need, Charlie?" he asks in an octave that I swear my channel is now programmed to respond to.

"I need…"

Shit. Am I actually asking? Am I honestly here in Rory's house, about to beg him for things I never sought to have?

Yes. I am. I know without a doubt that I am, and I can't for the life of me help it.

"I need to feel…how I felt…again. I need to know if…if I can feel like that again."

His hand falls from my face. He stuffs it in the pocket of his jeans. Have I surpassed the amount of time he's willing to spend on his flings? I'm probably the most boring and difficult partner he's ever had. He can just go to his club and handpick what kind of man he wants, like he's browsing a restaurant menu. Why the fuck would he want to waste time on me trying to come to terms with what my first cock cage did to me?

"I was just about to have dinner."

I want to shrink on the spot. It's nearly eight o'clock. That seems late for dinner to me, but it's not what makes me the most uncomfortable. The message is clear—his stomach is more important than the curiosity he's awoken in me. Turning, he starts toward his kitchen. My heart falls to the pit of my stomach, watching him go. I've never felt so foolish and completely dismissed.

Just as he passes under the archway, however, he stops and calls over his shoulder. "You'll find what you're looking for in the living room cabinet. If you want to get yourself ready, I'll join you in a few minutes."

I stare after him for a moment, confused. Turning, I hedge my way deeper into his house, curious about his instructions. Around the corner, I find a large bookcase with paneled glass doors, which I'm guessing is the cabinet he referred to, since there isn't anything else in here that fits the bill. To my right is a long, mirrored dining table, and near the opposite side of the room are a sofa and a coffee table. Scanning the cabinet contents, I see books and trinkets—bookends and small figurines that look to be from foreign countries. If he thinks I'm supposed to understand his riddle this time, he's going to be disappointed. I don't know what the fuck he's talking about, but then…I see it.

On the top right shelf, there's a wooden box a little longer and thicker than a brick. On the front of it is a silver placard with one word engraved on it—*Charlie*.

It's not. It can't be. Why would he…

Fingers trembling, I open the cabinet and slide the box off the shelf, setting it down on the ledge near my waist. Every ounce of frustration I've carried over the last few weeks evaporates as soon as I tilt the lid open. The familiar silver cage sits nestled in a custom-fitted bed of blue velour. Hanging from a small hook on the inside of the lid is the little key, its chain dangling from it.

He keeps it…in his living room? What if he has company and they see my name on the box?

I hear a beep sound from the kitchen and flinch. He said to get myself ready and that he'd join me in a few minutes.

Turning, I blink at the array of windows overlooking the back of his property. It's dim in here with just the soft glow from a few wall sconces. There are no neighbors behind his house, but the wide-open space is daunting. I keep my bedroom window curtains drawn at all times.

Glancing back at the box, I chew at the inside of my lip, hating the lightness to my cock and balls. That familiar feeling of weight, of…belonging, is within my reach. And there seems to be a willing man just a room away. I don't want to go back to struggling to get off to lackluster releases or that feeling of want without an erection. I want my life back, which includes my sex life, no matter how eccentric it was before Rory came along. I need to know.

Huffing, I kick my shoes off and shove my jeans and boxer briefs to the floor. This is so surreal—standing in the middle of a guy's living room that I've never been in, putting a cage on my own cock. Pinching my eyes closed, I slide my sac through the cable and the cage over my cock. I force the cable tighter, nudging it deeper into the empty spine of the cage until it's as tight as I remember it being before. Reaching underneath it, I slide some of the numbers until I hear them click, locking myself in.

Blowing out a breath, I stare down at the results of my efforts. The sight and sensation instantly arouse me. Yet, it's more than arousal. I feel…better. Safe. Cared for. Is it the reunion with my cage or Rory's promise to join me soon?

Suddenly, a wave of self-consciousness washes over me. It's brighter in here than it was in his cabin the last night of the cruise. I know there's an entire wall of windows and some late-night hiker could be out there, but I feel like a jackass in my sweatshirt and socks in his fancy living room. I don't want to look any more insecure than I already am. Whipping off my shirt, I toss it down onto my discarded pants and then tug off my socks. I tell myself it's because I've learned to be confident, not because of Rory's comment about my tank top having sand on it when I was in his cabin that night. I'm not here to please him. I'm here to learn how I like to be pleased.

"Are you hungry?" he asks, startling me.

Spinning around, instinct has my hands moving to cover myself, but I stop them at the last second. Flexing my fingers at my sides, I watch him make his way over to the coffee table with a serving tray. There's a rectangular ceramic dish on it, covered with a lid.

Shaking my head, I act like I'm appreciating the art on his walls. Dinner? Is he seriously going to eat dinner right now while I'm standing here bare-ass naked?

"I'm starving," he murmurs, setting the tray down on the end table next to the sofa.

Fuck. What do I do? Put my clothes back on while he eats? He insinuated I should get ready—wasn't getting caged and naked ready?

Walking over to the coffee table, he bends down and pats the surface, flashing me a smile. "Will you join me?"

Am I supposed to sit on his table with my bare ass while he eats? Inching forward, I try not to look as bewildered as I feel. When I'm within arm's reach, his eyes travel the length of my body, and he lets out a satisfied sound.

His hand goes to my biceps, and I turn when he urges me to, facing the coffee table. I feel like a marionette again as his hands make gentle movements, guiding me. In moments, I'm on my hands and knees on the little table, staring at his dormant big screen on the opposite wall. And then…he walks away. What the fuck is going on?

When I see his white shirt swish to the floor, it eases some of my nerves but frays new ones. He's going to deliver, after all. The zipper of his jeans follows. Soon they and his underwear join his shirt. The next thing I hear is the sound of the lid being removed from that ceramic dish. Is he going to fucking eat in the nude while I'm perched on his damn coffee table?

Sneaking a glance over my shoulder, I find him walking toward me with that oblong dish and what looks like a small pastry brush in his hand. There are two serving dishes inside the ceramic container, both filled with clear liquids. It's not food after all.

"You're going to like this, handsome. I promise."

Catching his pleased smile, I whip my head back around and swallow against the fluttering sensation that's crept up my windpipe. There's the Rory I know. The one who's always three steps ahead of me.

I feel his heat behind me. The outside of his thighs brush against the inside of my calves. Something soft and wet, almost like saturated feathers, slides between my cheeks. It's warm, so warm it's soothing, and the slick contact sends a flutter through my abdomen. I let out a puff of air and hang my head as he brushes back and forth through my crease.

He leaves. The clink of the dish returning to its tray pierces the silence, and then his warmth returns to the place between my feet. When his hands rest on the top of my ass and circle in a welcoming caress, my eyes slip closed. A current of relief trickles down my legs all the way to my toes, and the tension in my stomach uncoils. God, why do I love this so much?

"And here I thought I was going to be dining alone," he purrs.

I blink, wondering what the fuck he means, but then the lap of a tongue across my hole has my eyes slamming shut as the air is sucked out of my lungs. A chorus of filthy noises floats over my back—slurps and satisfied sounds that people make when they eat their favorite food.

Jesus, hell. I get it now. *I'm* his fucking dinner, and the menu is already going up in flames.

It's good, so good. That mouth, that tongue. It's what I've been missing. Those peculiar savoring little kisses to my hole like it's some precious thing to be revered. He follows them up with jabs of his tongue and then dives in, reuniting with my channel.

I'm rocking back against his face, fully aware of it this time. Fully unscathed by it. I don't care that this has never been me. It feels too right, too good. Through my graceless moans, I want to laugh. Maybe I did need dinner. I was starving for this, and Rory is satisfying that hunger.

"M-more. More," I chant, knowing I've just entered the greedy zone.

I should have learned by now. Every time I talk, he stops. His mouth leaves me, and I grunt a frustrated sound.

"More *what*, handsome?" he asks in that casual tone, sliding a hand up and down my ribs.

Fuck. He *knows*. I know he knows. Why does he have to ask?

I can wholeheartedly say I've learned one thing from this adventure of self-discovery. I still don't like begging. Getting rimmed? Yes, I love that. Wanting his thick cock to press through my ring? Yeah, that's what I want next. But asking for it—why does he do this to me?

Remembering how he rewards my '*bravery*,' I yield to the discomfort and speak. "You… Your…cock."

Holy shit, if I knew he was capable of making that deep, throaty growl, I wouldn't have just put myself through that mental lashing. He strokes his tip over my ring a few times, sending all my blood to my cinched balls. Fuck, this is what I've wanted, what I've desperately been trying to feel for weeks. I'm quaking for it.

"Only because you asked so nicely," he whispers, pushing against my hole.

I press back, too eager to care about looking wanton. My ring stretches, tearing a grunt from my throat. There's a burn, but it's worth it. My body gives way and swallows him, pulling him inside my heat.

Dropping my head, my voice falls out in a low chord, purging weeks of frustration. I'm speared, just the way I want to be. *Finally*.

His hands go to work making invisible designs with his touch all over my back and thighs as his hips begin their wicked tease. His cockhead passes over my gland, blooming a burst of electricity to my dick. I don't care if there's anyone in the woods outside right now. I don't care if anyone sees. Don't care if my noises scare away some wild animal. All that matters right now is what this man's cock does to me.

He surprises me with a quick thrust, sending him all the way home. My jaw falls open, my eyes wide. He's just emptied my brain with that bolt of bliss he shot through my core. It was more urgent, more feral than last time. Less delicate. And fuck, I didn't mind it at all. I don't mind the sound of approval he makes, either, knowing I caused that sound.

"Is that what you needed, Charlie?" he asks, sounding strained.

I just want to bask in the fullness, not answer questions. I'm home. I'm complete. In this fleeting moment, I have what I've been yearning for. Why does he have to ruin it?

I try to rock forward, but his grip on my hips tightens, keeping me tight against his groin. Son of a bitch. He really expects an answer?

"Yes!" I bark in frustration, but it comes out sounding more like a plea.

He answers the plea, drawing back and then thrusting home again. Whatever that speed and force did to my gland, to my channel, it reverberates through my entire being. He's just taken this game to a new level, and I have a feeling I'm well good and fucked in a new way—no pun intended. He was holding out on me last time, taking it easy on me.

The next ten minutes are filled with the slap of skin and unholy noises that I didn't know I was capable of. My elbows are about ready to give out, and I'm worried I cinched the cage cable too tight. The circulation to my cock is zilch at the moment. I'm so full. I've resorted to whining and mewling, hoping he knows it means I want to come before I pass the fuck out.

Bending over me, his palm cups my swollen balls, and his tongue draws a stripe up the side of my neck. "Fucking hell, Charlie. Do you feel that?" he pants. His hand draws off my sac and slides up to the side of my ass. It's gone, and then there's a rush of air. I hear a crack of skin to skin and a zing of static explodes in my ass cheek. It shoots right to my balls, which sets off that sweet internal explosion that sets my cock to erupting. "We fit so fucking good."

We do. Bloody hell, we do. I bellow, still high on that slap to my ass as my cock unloads and my channel spasms around him. His chest makes a rumbling noise, and his hips give a few frantic thrusts before he jerks against my ass, buried deep, and comes.

I come down in a haze as though I'm being slowly lowered from the top of a fifty-story building. It's that strange phenomenon of what was a drug-like high moments ago morphing into an awkward reality. His cock slips free of my hole, and I drip. The dreaded question pops into my head—now what?

The lights in the room, the wall of windows, everything comes back to me with vivid clarity. My clothes are feet away in a pile on the floor, warning me I'll have to dress in front of him.

He peels himself off my back and gives my hip a squeeze. I feel lips touch down on my ass, pressing a kiss there.

"Mm. You definitely improved my Saturday evening."

Um…nice.

Shit. I hate this part. This is why I'm a one-and-done guy. I don't know how to do small talk with guys. What's so wrong about just getting off and getting the hell out? There doesn't need to be words. I can talk, I just haven't ever felt a desire to. And with Rory…well, I have no fucking clue what the hell I should say to the CEO of the company I work for moments after I was begging for his dick.

Easing off the coffee table, I try to ignore the effect of his touch when he helps me by the arm. I don't think I'll ever get over his gentlemanly tendencies. Glancing down, I realize I have a decision to make. Part of me wants to take this cage home in case I'm still plagued with the urge to wear it again. Yet, it's not mine. I mean, Rory had it here in a box in his house, so I can't just assume it really was a gift. Jeez, listen to me—thinking of this thing as a gift after all the fuss I made.

Trying to lift my balls, I come to a standstill. I can't do the combination like this unless I hold a mirror underneath my sac. Fuck.

"Here, let me get that for you."

Fan-tastic. Standing still, I wait as my CEO gets to his knees and enters the combination. I'm tempted to ask him to confirm what the numbers stand for, but tell myself it doesn't matter. I'm convinced I will never understand Rory McDonnell or anything he does, even if I try. Besides, I'm more concerned with understanding myself.

Apparently, I now like to bottom. I like to bottom while wearing a cock cage. Research accomplished.

"I was serious about dinner," he remarks, getting to his feet and heading toward a door off the hallway, taking my filthy cage with him. "Have you eaten yet? I was just about finished in the kitchen. If you give me ten minutes, I can have a hot meal ready for us."

Is he serious? He wants to eat dinner together like nothing just happened…again?

"Uh…yeah. I ate earlier. But thanks." I dash to my clothes while his back is turned, but freeze with them in my hands, holding them over my junk when he turns around.

He holds my gaze with an indiscernible expression. The corner of his mouth finally ticks up along with his shoulder. "No worries."

When he disappears into the next room, I waste no time dressing. I'm sure plenty of people can have casual encounters and fuck buddies. Hell, I had a fuck buddy in college for a semester.

I'm also sure, however, that most people aren't fuck buddies with their boss. This ends tonight. I got the answers I came for.

As I tie my shoes, a twisted voice inside my head mocks me. *You mean you came for the answers that you got?*

Rory returns, striding past me, naked as a jaybird. He walks over to the cabinet. I slow my lacing as an excuse to see what he plans on doing with the cage. There aren't any other boxes in that cabinet, now that I think about it. That shouldn't please me. It doesn't mean he hasn't had other boxes in there before tonight.

I hear the lid slam shut, and he turns around, holding it out to me with a smile. I stare for several awkward seconds before I accept it. Does this mean he's done with me? I want things to be done with him. It's just that it would be kind of fucked up if he wanted them done too, since he went to so much trouble and flair to make it happen.

"You left it on the ship, so I took the liberty of bringing it home for you. Seems like you might want to use it in the future."

I plan on saying something. I even open my mouth to do so. For as much as I've complained about him, he's being very…understanding and maybe even generous. I'm not coming back, and I think he knows it. It feels like he's letting me off the hook easily, and yet, I don't think there's a catch. For once, there's no playful remark, no riddle, no repercussions. He's literally leaving the decision in my hands in the form of this box and its contents.

I close my jaw, realizing nothing is going to come. This was certainly one hell of an experience, a tale I could tell someone years from now and they'd never believe it. I flash him a flicker of a smile with the corner of my mouth and then nod.

"Goodnight." It's all I can manage, but it will have to do.

I walk to the door with the box in my hand. I carry it all the way out to the Porsche sitting in his driveway. And then I drive home, ignoring how absurd it is to enjoy the feeling of his come seeping out of my ass, but doing so anyway, since it's the last time it's ever going to happen.

CHAPTER 15

Three months later

My forehead bashes into the drywall in Rory's entryway. He didn't even take me into the living room this time. He had me strip right here just inside his doorway and then spun me around, dropped to his knees, and spread my cheeks to whisper filthy things to my hole before he got down to business. When is this going to stop?

I should be embarrassed that I'm over here again, but as his cockhead nudges through my ring, I feel no shame. I even like the way he's still fully dressed this time. It makes me imagine we just left a meeting, and he's got me pinned up against a wall at head-quarters. I have nothing to be embarrassed about if he doesn't seem to mind that I showed up again.

At least, I've never used the key. Not the one for the cage, but the other one I found beneath the cage when I got home from his house the first time I came over. It's a key to his house. I know it is without needing confirmation. A thousand bucks said he put it in there just to tempt me. It was a silent invitation that was louder than any bullhorn. Two weeks later, I fucking took that invitation like a damn Rory sex addict. And I've been taking it at least every other weekend since that first night. It's getting worse, though.

This is the second time this week. I was just here Wednesday night—the first time I folded during the work week. Now, it's Sat-urday night. Another weekend night where guys my age are out doing normal things like finding a boyfriend, seeing a concert, or watching a game. But no, not me. What am I doing? Scratching an itch that only gets itchier each time I come to Rory to scratch it.

Fuck. I think I truly am starting to hate him. I'm worried I've lost any hope of another man arousing me at this point. And my hand? Dildos? Well, my body knows they're not Rory. Why does it have to be *him* I crave?

He rocks slowly back and forth over my gland at least a dozen times. I want him deep. I want to be completely filled. I want him seated all the way until I can feel that soft patch of hair at his groin brushing up against my taint. I'm about to give in to begging again, when suddenly I'm empty.

"Mm," he hums, kneading one of my cheeks. "That was wonderful."

Um…yeah, so why did he stop? Did he come? I'm pretty sure he didn't.

He gives my ass a little swat. Not too hard, not too soft—just the way I like it.

Panting, I watch him peel his sweatshirt over his head and drop it on the floor. Turning, he starts down the hallway but doesn't make his way into the living room. Where the fuck is he going?

I hear the zip of his fly, and his blue jeans slide down his legs. Licking my lips, I admire the sight of him going commando. Just as he rounds the corner, he calls out, "Are you coming?"

Heaving a breath, I push off the wall and follow him. I love how he says shit, like I'm supposed to know where the hell I'm going. We've only ever fucked in his living room or that one time in the kitchen when he bent me over one of the stools.

When I round the corner, I freeze in the open doorway. I've never seen the door open. If I had, I would have known it was a bedroom. A very sizable bedroom with a slightly raised, carpeted platform in the middle of it.

In the center of that platform is a king-size bed, and currently crawling onto that exquisite-looking bed is one naked Rory McDonnell. When his ass touches down on the mattress and he settles back against the pillows, I stare at his glistening cock, pointed toward the ceiling.

I tell myself that it doesn't matter that it's a bedroom or that he's on a bed. We fucked on a bed once before on his yacht. If I make some protest, he'll just tease me, and I'm too turned out to ruin it right now. I spot a switch on the wall by the doorway and dim the lights, then make my way over to him. He has what I need right now. Who cares if he changed the venue?

Except, just as I take a knee on the mattress and make to assume my usual position, he grabs my arm and tugs. With his other hand, he pats the top of his thigh.

"Right here, handsome," he informs me.

How the fuck is that going to work? Does he want my ass in his face again? He already put lube all over me. He had a packet in his pocket like he was expecting me, the smug bastard. I swear he made me attend that luncheon the other day with the contracting department because he knew I'd cave sooner if I had to see him in person. And I did. I told myself I'd skip what's becoming our regular Saturday night ritual, but… Well, here I am. I'll think about how weak my willpower is later.

Moving to turn and face the end of the bed, so I can sling my leg over the top of his, I wobble when he tugs on my arm again with more force. Why is he laughing?

Twisting around, I'm sure my face shows my confusion, especially when he plants his other hand on my hips and drags me closer to him. I have no choice but to move my knee so I don't faceplant on his chest.

"You're so cute. You know that?" he purrs, and I find myself straddling him. Straddling him as I *face him*. What the actual fuck?

Gripping the headboard for balance, I hold my breath while I assess the situation. There's enough light in here that nothing will be left to the imagination. I've never looked at him while we mess around. I've hardly looked at him at all, to be honest. At least, not while he's looking back at me. This is so weird. He can't possibly want to fuck like this. What's wrong with what we've been doing? Am I getting too boring for him?

Fuck. Each time I come here, I swear it's the last, but each time I leave, I know that's a lie. It was never supposed to go on this long.

When he reaches between my legs, grabs his cock, and rubs his tip back and forth through my crease, a sliver of worry needles at me. I'm worried about my sanity because I'm instantly curious to see how it would feel to slide down on his cock while it's at that angle. I bet I'd get him deeper than when he's behind me. Damn it. He really has broken me.

CHAPTER 16

Rory

Watching the emotions that flicker across Charlie's face is always
a thing of awe. Watching them face-to-face while I drag my cockhead over his slickened hole—the most entrancing thing I've ever
seen. And yet, slightly heartbreaking.

God, if he would just let himself go. I can't imagine the way the
passion would seep through his features. I want to see it so badly,
but I refuse to push him.

His eyes slip shut and stay pinched closed. A little huff leaves
his lips. It sounds equal parts sexual frustration and stage fright,
but he's not made a move to get off my lap. He looks so good in
my bed, so good on top of me. If he knew how many times I've
dreamt about this, he'd probably up and run out of here the way
he does each time we've finished enjoying each other. All I can
do is hope. Hope and please him as best I can. So, that's exactly
what I set about doing.

Running a hand up his thigh, I stroke the soft skin at the juncture of his hip and then glide my palm back down over his flexed
muscles. I can feel him soften beneath my touch, relaxing because of my hand. I love the way he responds to a delicate touch.
So gruff on the exterior and yet, so quickly yielding to the kind of
intimacy I long to give him.

A shadow of conflict flashes across his face. Biting his lower
lip, he turns his head to the side, and I feel him push against me.
I stare unabashedly at his face as he lowers himself onto me,

waiting for the second those lips part at the feel of me. The little groans he makes and the way his body slowly cuffs me have my own eyes slipping closed. *Fuck*. He's so perfect.

Whatever his hang-ups are that prevented him from bottoming before no longer make me sad for him at this moment. I'm too grateful for the knowledge that I'm the only man he's trusted enough to take. I like knowing I'm the only one he's taken. Call me possessive, but I accepted long ago that's what Charlie North does to me.

I haven't for a minute imagined he hasn't at least tried with someone else. The way he looked so distraught, nearly deranged, when he first showed up at my house three months ago, I could tell. He'd been experimenting. I hated the thought of him experimenting with someone else—even himself—but I know it's what he needed. I shouldn't have been so happy to deduce that he probably hadn't had it in him to go through with anything with another person. I could tell just by how jittery he was, how tight he still was. It was like every touch I gave him was brand new, more firsts he'd been experiencing. I wanted to devour him the second I walked into my living room and found him ready and waiting for me, silently asking.

The bottom of his ass touches down on the top of my thighs. His constricted balls, so ripe and full, settle on my navel. I close my eyes and inhale a deep breath at the heat and pressure of him encasing me. I need a moment or three for a sensation like this.

I can feel the puffs of breath venting over me and wonder if he's looking, if he's curious to see us joined in this position. I knead his thigh and let loose one little groan. It's always a constant struggle to hold back. If I didn't, I know it would be too much for him. He's not ready to learn just how much I want him. Maybe he never will be, but for now, I'm content with keeping my full desire locked away.

Whatever he feels or sees is enough to get him over his anxiety about changing things up. He moves, just in fragments at first, riding me in tiny undulations. I can't *not* watch, so I open my eyes, but keep them focused on where we're joined. I know my Charlie is too shy to have a witness to the passion on his face. It's what did me in the first time I saw this sexy, confident-looking man at that convention last year, quietly checking other men out. I'd decided to make the rounds to a few conventions, covertly observing the company's top performers, and was already curious about tracking him down. It's funny now that I was always intrigued by how articulate his emails were that I'd been cc'd on over the years, and the way he adds the salutation, '*Respectfully yours,*' at the end of each of them. As soon as I caught him quietly ogling that gaggle of attractive convention goers, however, what looked good on paper became ten times better in reality. That blush on his cheeks and the flicker of his pulse in his neck when I spoke to him made me want to whisk him away and cover his mouth with mine. I wasn't sure if he'd even show up at my club, to be honest.

When Silas, the club's security guard, called to let me know, I was pleasantly surprised. I waited, though. I waited, and I watched, curious about how my employee would find his experience at Illusion. I never review video footage from the club anymore. I have a manager and security people for that, but I couldn't help myself. Once I saw what I saw, I was doomed. A prisoner to everything that is Charlie North.

From his anxiousness, his wholesome reactions, and even the bewildered little smiles he made after each of his visits—how his serious façade would return and he'd button himself up—I couldn't stand not experiencing that from the other side of the panel. Before I even dropped to my knees that first night, I think I knew I was going to be a goner. Once I did, well, it just became nothing short of an obsession.

God, he was so beautiful. If I'd seen who it was that worked for me all these years, I'd never have gotten anything done.

His hips raise up higher this time, and then drop back down. The sound he makes is another song of discovery that has me preening. He's such a maddening contradiction—all gruff denial and bottled-up passion. Fuck, I love being responsible for making him feel good.

He rocks again and then again, spanking my pelvis with the bottom of his. One hand is still gripping my headboard, and he drops the other in a fist to my pillow and groans. How I wish he weren't afraid to touch me. At least, he seems to be over his hesitancy about riding my cock, thrusting back down again with more vigor. It creates a balloon of delicious pressure in my abdomen and balls. I'm so glad I jerked off before he came over, or I'd be disappointing him right now. I want him to enjoy this to the fullest, and I'm grateful I was right about his anticipated visit tonight.

"*Yess,*" I hiss. "Just like that."

It's taking everything in me to keep my gaze averted from his. I do the only other thing I can, snaking my hands up his torso and chest, mapping the feel of his skin. The way his stomach flexes under my touch is a heady connection to his movements. Reaching back up, I stroke my fingertip around one of his nipples. He lets out a strangled sound and tenses. Not just his body, but his channel. It grips me tight, a telling sign.

I do glance up now, unable to miss witnessing this moment. With his neck arched back and his mouth open, he moans, coming through his cage and onto my stomach. If he were a dessert, I'd eat him alive right now. I swear.

Sitting up, I reach underneath his shoulders and grip him. Flipping him down to the mattress on his back, I trail my hands up his arms and weave his fingers into mine. Drawing my hips back, I tug my cock from his greedy pulses and instead focus on kissing his gasping throat. The strained cords there are too great a temptation not to appreciate. As I settle between his legs, his chest and stomach heave against mine with each of his spent breaths. I love him like this—completely wasted with pleasure. He's so soft and open during these moments. It's what I imagine he'd be like if he could ever free himself of the unnecessary weight he insists on carrying.

When I move my mouth to the place over his thumping heartbeat, I can't resist any longer. Scooting my hips closer, I drag my cock between his cheeks until it finds that warm opening. His fingers tighten around mine where our hands are joined. I find him gazing at me in confusion. Shit, he's adorable.

He can leave any time. I've made sure he knows this. Even if he comes first and doesn't want to witness me enjoying his body. I take my chances, though, giving his hands a squeeze as I press forward.

"No," I confirm in front of his gaping mouth. "I'm not done with you yet, Charlie."

I have to turn my head when he gasps before I'm too tempted to swallow it. His cage brushes against my abdomen as I seat myself deep inside him. When I groan, he groans with me. I hide my smile in his neck and take a hit of his scent, basking in the way his body hugs me.

Sliding my calves up underneath my thighs, I nudge his legs further apart. They move awkwardly at first, but then he lets them settle over the top of mine. Charlie, my brave Charlie.

I move then, unable to remain still in his body's death grip on my cock any longer. The little whimpering sounds he makes with each slow thrust have me feeling carnal. I nibble his earlobe, suck on it, and pepper kisses on the side of his neck. They're all a preview of what I want to do to the mouth making those wonderful noises.

His hips start moving, rocking up into mine. His chest undulates against my own as though he wants more skin-to-skin contact. He's going positively rabid beneath me, his head thrashing from side to side. When I feel his legs rise and his feet lock around the back of my waist, I have to bite my lip to keep from cursing.

"Rory... Uhn, s-so good."

Hearing him moan my name when he's all but wrapped around me is the last straw. I find his mouth and silence his praises with my lips. He goes rigid beneath me, but I need a taste before he decides to stop.

"God damn it, Charlie," I pant, staring down into his big blue eyes. "I've tried. I've tried so fucking hard. I'm sorry."

Licking the seam of his lips, they open to me. I groan the second I feel the silk of his mouth and his tongue against mine. He whimpers, and it's like a rubber band gave way, with all the tension draining from his body. Someone, please save me—Charlie has become a puddle beneath me.

His hands slip from mine and grip the back of my shoulders. The paralysis in his mouth subsides, and he starts kissing me back. I dig my fingers into his hair and grip a handful of it.

Yes... He's everywhere, cocooning me in my favorite thing—*him*. I feast on his mouth and pound into him, ravenous. Not a single one of his noises reaches the air. I swallow them all as I fuck them out of him, like I'm racking up points in a video game.

Like all good things, though, it ends too soon. I have to tear my mouth away to breathe as I come. Staring down at him while I groan, I watch the wonder in his expression as he watches me. I want to kiss that look right off his face and tell him he can watch this any time he wants to. He's just like Jeremy, so much that it breaks my heart.

Collapsing on top of him, I lie in the silence, trying to catch my breath. As I rest here against Charlie's warm body, I wonder if I have a thing for sheltered cases. Maybe I have for years. Even before Jeremy took his life when we were teens, I always looked out for guys who were ashamed of their sexuality. I was never ashamed, and I wanted them to know the freedom I felt. I wanted my friend to know he didn't have to pretend to be straight just because society wasn't as accepting back then. Look at me—I did all right, being who I am. Jeremy never got to know that. I just hope to hell Charlie figures it out too, even if it's not with me.

Rolling to my side to take my weight off him, I know the second I glance over at him that it's a lie. I really want it to be with me. He's not some charity case, or some closeted gay man I feel I have to save. He's just...who I want. I've seen glimpses of his humor. I've seen the way he carries himself around his peers. I'm in awe of his work ethic and his mind. I love his grit, even if I do like that it crumbles when he's around me. Being in awe of the rest of him, though, was just a pleasant surprise.

I stare, waiting for him to open his eyes, but he doesn't. Not that I'm looking forward to finding out if he'll up and leave like his ass is on fire as usual, but I expect it. Except this time, his breathing evens out. One arm at his side, the other lounging near his head on the pillow, his lips part with a stream of breath. He's...sleeping.

I smile with a puff of laughter. Now that's a delightful sight. Brushing my thumb along his jaw, I whisper, "Charlie...you're not going to run out on me tonight?"

He grunts an annoyed sound as though he's perturbed I've interrupted his sleep, and yet, he turns his head toward my touch like he wants me to stay close. He's going to be the death of me, I swear. Leaning over, I place a soft kiss on his lips. If anything can get him to reconnect with his fight-or-flight response, it will surely be a kiss, judging by the way he looked when I first tasted his mouth a little while ago. I don't want him to regret anything or think I tricked him into staying. As my lips dust his, however, he lets out a sleepy little moan.

Charlie in my bed for the night it is, then. I'm certainly not going to complain.

I go to the bathroom and wet a cloth, returning to find him on his side, hugging my pillow underneath his head. "Settled right in, didn't you?" I murmur.

I do my best to gently clean him up. When I get to his cage, though, I cringe. How long is he going to think he needs it?

I have yet to see him come to me without it once. I suspect for him it's like a child's teddy bear, bringing him a false sense of comfort for the things he fears. Charlie is, without a doubt, a man who needs an excuse to experience intimacy—something he can blame for letting his hair down.

As I turn out the lights and slide into bed behind him, I can't help but wonder if there's more to it. Is it the letting go he fears, or is it me?

CHAPTER 17

Charlie - Three weeks later

Fuck. I need to see him.

Not because I want to, but because I have to. The news I overheard about the Divine family considering selling is too big to pass up. If Amor acquired their company, we'd be an international chocolate empire. Rory would want in on that, right? Never mind how amazing it would be if I were the guy to make it happen— that's not the point.

Staring across the parking lot at headquarters, I tell myself to just grip the car door handle and open it. Nothing happens, though.

"Who cares? You've been working under him for months now, and you both manage it just fine," I reassure myself aloud.

I try to ignore how that phrase '*working under him*' always makes my cock stir. But I've managed it…sort of. Well, *he* manages it just fine. I've been struggling to be honest.

Anytime I have to interact with him, whether it be via email or in person, it's like I lose all common sense and become a scatter-brained airhead. And the bitch of it is that I know why. It's because I haven't had a fix of him in three weeks. It's killing me. It shouldn't be, but it is.

That was the last time, Charlie. I repeat the words to myself, hoping the message sinks in this time.

He…*kissed me*. And I…kissed him back. A lot.

And then I fell asleep, and I'm pretty sure he cleaned me up. We…slept together in the same bed. All night. I saw his sleeping face in the morning when I woke up, curled into him like a baby kangaroo, gripping onto its mother. Things were getting way too complicated.

I thought I could just sneak out, but no. I'm not that lucky. He sat up with sexy bedroom hair and offered to cook me breakfast. Breakfast! Like…like a boyfriend or something.

What would I do with a boyfriend? What would my brothers say if I had a boyfriend? How would I work for a boyfriend?

See! Complicated. Way too fucking complicated.

"It's a three-billion-dollar deal, Charlie," I inform myself. "Just get out of the car, march in there, and *do not* stare at his mouth or think with your ass."

Wrenching the door open, I move on pure willpower toward the entrance. I hope it doesn't run out before I get to the third floor. By the time I make it to Rory's assistant's desk, I'm trembling and want to throw up.

He greets me chipperly, and an ugly thought clouds my brain. Has Rory fucked him? Does he *want* Rory to fuck him?

Ugh. I hate this.

Luckily, he tells me I can go in. I want to snort and inform him I don't need permission to storm in and see the man I let fuck me, but I haven't lost all my marbles just yet. As soon as I'm inside and the door closes behind me, however, my piss and vinegar dissolve. I hate how the sight of him is like a damn sedative to my system. It turns me into some dopey-eyed, smitten fool as though he's an aphrodisiac.

"Charlie," he greets from his desk chair, looking way too good in a dress shirt and tie. I want to tear it off with my teeth and ask him to tie my hands up with it.

Jesus fucking Christ. What is wrong with me?

"I didn't know you were in the neighborhood today," he adds, tossing a file to the side.

"I…I wanted to discuss something with you," I manage, taking a few steps closer.

He motions to the chair on the opposite side of his desk, but I forgo the offer. Instead, I stuff my hands in my pockets and look out the line of windows in his office.

"I got good information that the Divine family is considering selling. They're supposed to be at the Confectionery Expo in Salzburg next week. I was thinking if…if Amor were interested in buying them, I could try to get a meeting with them."

Glancing over anxiously, I try to assess his reaction. Hands folded in front of his mouth, he just watches me, listening. I have an audience, the kind that doesn't make me nervous. I know business, and I especially know *this* business.

"I know acquisitions aren't in my new job description, but I've met them a few times over the years, and they've always been receptive to me, so…so I thought it was worth mentioning…or… offering. If…if that's something you'd want to do."

I hear an amused sound that has my spine going rigid in mortification, but then he says, "Are you kidding me? I'm certainly not going to say no if the Divines are thinking about selling. Are you sure, though? How reliable is your information?"

"Dexter Divine's best friend plays racquetball at the gym I go to. She said his mother is sick and that he's more interested in his Formula 1 career."

How lovely to be so rich that you can fund your own racing line. I watch surprise take over his face as he lowers his hands and leans back in his chair.

"You play racquetball?"

How is *that* what he's concerned with right now? And, yes, I play racquetball. Lately, I've played a lot of racquetball because playing racquetball is the closest thing I can find to alleviating my sexual frustrations, short of storming back over to his house and whatever awaits me there. Probably more kisses. More deep, slow, toe-curling kisses that make me feel like I can't breathe and terrify the shit out of me, but in a way that I also don't exactly want the terror to stop.

Oh, for fuck's sake. Stop it, Charlie.

"A bit," I digress, deciding I can offer a response since we're clothed, and it won't cost me a part of my soul.

"Hm. I guess I bet on the right horse," he says, focusing on a pen as he rolls it back and forth with his fingers. "Well, if you're asking for my permission to make me billions of dollars, you have it. I'll have Scott book you a flight right away. Take as long as you need. If you can make this happen, you won't just be changing the company, you'll be changing your life too."

I'm not sure what that means, but I suspect it entails more of his generosity. How much more generous can you get than a Porsche and my already tripled salary?

"I just…want to make it happen." I shrug.

Smiling, he assures me, "And I have no doubt you will."

That was easier than I thought, except now that I've got what I wanted, I need something else. I was silently hoping he'd tell me he had no interest in acquiring Divine. It would have been much easier to stay focused on our marketing branches here in the States. Heading off to Europe, though, for this expo, and then who knows how long I'll have to wait to get a meeting with Dexter, then negotiations if I can make it happen—I could be gone for weeks. Gone to another country far away from Rory.

"Was there something else?" he asks patiently.

I want the floor to swallow me up. Seriously, sometimes I think it would be easier to just go to therapy to find out why my brain has been thinking about the things it has lately. The chain and key are probably as sweaty as my hand is in my pocket right now. Shuffling forward, I keep my gaze on my feet and then his desk when it comes into view. Reaching out, I open my palm and hold my breath, my face burning at what a fucked-up mess I am.

He must think I'm insane, standing here holding out the key to my cock cage for him in the middle of a workday in broad daylight. I can't go away that far and for that long without it, though, without knowing it's locked and he's the only one who can open it. I just can't do it after already denying myself of him for the last three weeks. I need…something to comfort me. Something to keep my libido in check so my brain can be on task. It's surreal how, when I first wore this thing, it consumed all my thoughts. Now, whenever I wear it, it makes me more confident. I'm going to need that confidence and focus to seal this deal.

After what feels like an eternity, I feel his fingers brush the palm of my hand, retrieving the key. I hope he didn't hear my little gasp of relief.

"You'll be great, Charlie. Don't worry."

My gaze flicks over to him with that bit of encouragement. It's the last thing I expected to hear. He says nothing more but gives me an understanding smile that makes me feel…*not abnormal* for what I just did. I nod, more grateful than embarrassed that he gets it. And then I leave, feeling ready to take on the world and more restored the farther away I get from that key and the man holding it.

CHAPTER 18

Charlie

It was only three weeks ago that I arrived in Salzburg for the expo, but it feels like a lifetime. My conversation with Dexter Divine while there led to landing a meeting with him, as I had hoped. That meeting produced an invitation to the Divine family estate in Bordeaux, France, where I met his mother and sister and learned about the family history of their company. Apparently, parting with a namesake was more difficult for them emotionally than I anticipated. They needed to know Divine would be going to a company that would appreciate their past. As I sat in their home overlooking the river Garonne, I assured them that Rory McDonnell is the type of man who appreciates special things, and that Amor would treat the Divine line with the respect it deserves. I don't think either promise was a lie. Dexter and his family, fortunately, didn't either and agreed to sell. Unfortunately, a business deal this size wasn't as simple as tying up over handshakes.

Grudgingly, I accompanied Dexter to a week's worth of his Formula 1 practice trials, while our acquisitions departments respectively drafted the appropriate contracts. It's been a wild ride of more foreign travel over the past month than I've experienced in my entire life. I've enjoyed seeing new places, but I'll be happy to get back to Portland.

Sitting across the dinner table from Dexter and his sister, I'm still busy enjoying it. Or at least pretending to. We're at a luxe restaurant tucked away just off Rue Saint-Rémi, celebrating that we'd finalized the sale contracts earlier today. I assume Rory wouldn't care if I put the bill on my corporate black card, but Dexter and his sister insisted it was their treat. Considering how much Rory is paying for their company, I didn't argue.

It has to be nearly morning back in Portland. As Betina gets up to excuse herself to the restroom, Dexter gets snared in conversation by an associate of his who walks by our table. I steal the silent moment to wonder how Rory feels waking up as the world's most renowned chocolate company owner. I'm sure his face will be on a few front pages of business magazines in the coming months once the word spreads. He'll have the world at his fingertips more so than he already does. Strangely enough, I have the suspicion he won't care. Give him a good book and a well-crafted cocktail, and he'd probably be happier. Smiling to myself over the insider knowledge, I frown when my spark of joy starts turning to wistfulness.

Rubbing my eyes does little to eradicate the tipsiness from the bottle of champagne he had sent to our table. I'll admit I felt a bit slighted at Dexter's laugh of delight upon its arrival when he read the attached note. *He* got a note, and I got nothing. Apparently, he spoke to Rory on the phone after the signing and must have alerted him to our dinner plans. Rubbing at the edge of my dessert plate, I'm fully aware it means Dexter also got a phone call, while I did not.

For a second, when the bottle arrived, I actually held my breath, wondering if a certain dark-haired man would follow. I've done admirably without him these past few weeks and am grateful I had the foresight to wear my cage for the trip. It's obviously helped. My sex drive has, surprisingly, been close to nil. The ache deep inside my chest, however, is something new that I've had plenty of time to contemplate. Through dinners, staring at race cars zipping by, and long, aimless walks down foreign streets, I've had ample time to come up with all manner of excuses.

The short of it is that I miss him. I still can't believe that I do, but the more I get familiar with the words rolling around inside my head, the truer they become.

I tried consoling myself with the champagne, telling myself it meant he was here in spirit. Dexter got champagne, a note, and a phone call. All I got was a cage…because that's all I asked for. I can't fight the niggling curiosity that if I'd ever asked for more, I would have gotten it. I know I could call him, but I feel like I need an excuse, and that he'd see through any excuse I come up with. What would I even say?

I called you because…even though I've acted like I want noth-ing to do with you, I wanted to hear your voice.

I can't sit here in a daze any longer, exchanging polite banter with Dexter and Betina. I'm not even sure if I've answered them with engaging responses all evening. I'm too distracted. Rory did give me something else, nothing personal, but something else.

Twenty percent…

When we signed the contracts today, the breakdown on future sales of Divine products had twenty percent going to me. The man from our legal department in our European office who flew in to oversee the signing assured me, *'It was written exactly as Mr. McDonnell specified.'*

I don't doubt it wasn't an error. But why would he do that? Is he paying me off?

After I left headquarters last month, I started thinking that the parting look he gave meant he understood all the things going on in my head that even I don't understand. I even kind of started thinking that maybe it meant he'd… I don't know. Put up with me for as long as I want him to put up with me? The Porsche felt like an invitation. This…this silence and payout don't.

Sighing, I pinch my eyes closed and pull my phone out of my pocket to see what time it is. Why am I playing devil's advocate when I still don't know what in the hell I want? I miss getting dicked by a certain man. *Whoop-dee-doo!* That's a far cry from having my shit figured out. Rory can't possibly miss me. I know I like the crazy shit he says sometimes, but there's no way a guy like him is going to waste his time flattering a guy like me much longer.

Clicking on my phone, I see several missed messages and calls. Crap. I put it on silent during the signing and haven't checked it since.

Legal sent me links to the finalized contracts. The knowledge that my bank account will soon explode should bolster more ex-citement, but I move on, unaffected. My mother sent a message reminding me to only drink bottled water so I don't get sick, be-cause she must think everywhere besides America is a third-world country with unclean resources. The dreaded group chat with my brothers is filled with mind-numbing chatter about their workouts, an upcoming barbecue, and how one of my nephews got sent to the principal's office again. Miles, my next oldest brother, at least acknowledged that I'm away, asking that I bring him back an air freshener in the shape of the Eiffel Tower. Minus two points to him for not realizing there are more cities in France than just Paris.

Feeling the need to reinforce my importance in the food chain, I rattle off a message to the group.

Just negotiated the sale of the world's largest chocolate company.

MILES: I hope that means I'll be getting a lifetime supply of candy bars to go with my air freshener.

Idiot. Shaking my head, I close out of the text thread before I'm bombarded with more sarcasm. Scrolling down, I spot one more message. My thumb stills over the screen name. *Rory—personal cell.* It's from earlier in the day. He sent me a message, and the frenetic butterflies in my stomach know it.

I'm so fucking proud of you. You'd better be celebrating tonight. You earned this.

"Finally, I think the champagne has worked!" Betina laughs.

I find her looking my way as she returns to her seat and realize her comment was directed at me. It takes me a second because I don't think I'm drunk, nor have I done anything that would make her think so, but then I realize I'm smiling. I try to stop, but can't, which makes me chuckle and produces another laugh from Betina.

"You have a good boss, I think," she remarks, holding her flute up to toast against mine. "Our company will be in good hands. I can tell."

I know she was referring to Rory sending the champagne, but all I can think of, as I agree with her, is that he is good, and so are his hands. I miss those hands. I miss those hands that sent me the most wonderful message from his personal phone.

Maybe…things could be different when I get back to Portland. Maybe his twenty percent wasn't a payoff to get rid of his flavor of the month after all. Maybe I'm not a flavor of the month and never was. But again, I'm looking at things from the wrong perspective. What am *I* willing to offer Rory?

When trying to find the answer makes me an anxious bundle of nerves, I say my goodbyes for the evening before my mood ruins the merriment. I walk back to the hotel the company put me up in and find myself in the shower, thinking about my CEO once again.

I've never showered with another man. There's a long list of things I've never done with a partner and for no good reason. I've never been on a date. Never held hands in public. Never gone to a movie. I've only taken and given very little in return, all in as much secrecy as I could capture.

I can say I'm busy, that I work too much, or that I'm afraid of what my family would think all I want, but they're all lies. I think the real reason I never contemplated having a boyfriend is that I know I'm not boyfriend material. I wouldn't know how to be even if I wanted to. Perhaps it's just wishful thinking. Some delusional part of me yearning for a life I never fathomed before, but sometimes I suspect Rory may want a boyfriend. He'd certainly be a generous and entertaining one. Extravagant gifts, home cooking, trips on his super yacht, and heated late-night sessions accompanied by heady words. But what would I do? Have a panic attack at the thought of stepping on his yacht alone with him in broad daylight or holding his hand as we walk into a restaurant? Boyfriends don't leave right after sex. Boyfriends spend the night, and eat home-cooked breakfast the next morning.

Leaning my head against the shower wall, I close my eyes against hot tears. There's also his adventurous side, which, although it excites me, I should probably accept that it's just my luck that the first person I'm considering is someone I can't keep up with. Boyfriends don't go to private clubs for blow jobs or put cock cages on people. I want something that doesn't exist. The club's name said it all. It was just an illusion. I'm in hell, a hell where I'm caught between a dream I'm not qualified enough to be the star of and one where I'm just adequate enough to pass the time with what I stumbled upon. I wish I'd never accepted that card from him.

CHAPTER 19

Rory

Swiping the key card over the lock, I push the hotel suite door open. My lungs are burning in anticipation of what I'll find. I know Europeans eat dinner and stay out later than the average American, but it's already midnight. Knowing Charlie, he's probably already tucked into bed, despite my encouragement to go out and enjoy his victory. The flight I caught couldn't get here fast enough, but it was the best I could do when I only got confirmation from legal this morning that the sale was officially going through today. Dexter's always been difficult to get to pin down dates, ever distracted by his whimsies and making plans last minute. I don't envy whatever Charlie had to go through to undertake this task.

Easing into the room, I find myself smiling at the dimly lit space. Only one bedside lamp on in the entire penthouse suite—yeah, Charlie is definitely here. Lowering my bag from my shoulder, I set it down quietly on the bench by the doorway when I hear noise from the bathroom. A flicker of anxiety pulses through my veins as I wait for him to emerge. Is this how he felt each time we were together?

I couldn't stay away any longer. Charlie has more layers than I realized. Asking me to hold the key for him, single-handedly brokering the largest confectionery acquisition in history—he amazes me at every turn. I didn't delude myself into thinking I'd get a call or message from him. Well, maybe I did, but each time I longed to hear his voice or see his face, I reminded myself that he gave me that key before he left. He was on a much-needed journey of self-discovery that would have been wrong of me to interrupt. My pulse is skittering erratically, waiting to see where the journey took him, but I couldn't fight my selfishness today. I need to see his face and congratulate him in person.

He steps out of the bathroom, barefoot in a white robe. Hair damp from a shower, his profile somber, the sight of him steals my breath and eases the weeks of longing in my chest. I adjust my grip on the flower bouquet in my hand so that the crinkle of their plastic sleeve will alert him to my presence.

He gives a start and turns toward me. Those bright blue eyes, wide in surprise, have dark circles under them and a hint of red to his whites. I want to go to him and tell him I'm a cure for sleepless nights, but hold myself back.

"Rory..." he stammers, leaving his jaw hanging open.

I can't fight my smile. "You did it."

The corner of his mouth ticks up, and he tucks his robe tighter around him, looking adorably self-conscious. "Um. Yeah. I did."

Stepping closer, I hold out the roses and drink him in. He looks at them like they're made of glass, taking them from me as though he's not sure he should.

"What...what are you doing here?"

Does he realize it's the first time he's looked at me while speaking since that first day on the yacht? It tells me everything I need to know—there's still hope.

"Did you think I could stand the thought of you here all alone with how fucking proud I am of you after what you just pulled off?"

His cheeks go pink, and his gaze drops immediately to the flowers. When his teeth bite into his lower lip, I cup his face and brush his cheek with my thumb, hoping he'll stop abusing himself over one well-deserved little compliment. "The way you blush for me will never get old. I don't even want to know if that means no one's ever told you all the wonderful things you need to hear."

His chest heaves on a gasp, but his eyes come back to me. "You...you gave me twenty percent."

There's a lost, vulnerable look in his expression that's a veritable magnet to my heart. Leaning in, I brush my lips over his and murmur. "I should have given you more."

"What? Why?"

"It was your deal, Charlie. I don't need the money." I can't remember the last time I felt self-conscious around someone, but maybe that's what he needs to see. Moving my hands to his hips, I draw closer and press another kiss to the corner of his mouth, still in awe that he's letting me. "I was being selfish because I was worried that if I gave you more, you might quit on me."

He scoffs and his face goes bright red, but he doesn't move away. Reaching one hand up, he strokes one of the flower buds with his thumb and mumbles, "Twenty percent isn't selfish."

I watch his nervous reverence of the flowers, and the way he can't bring himself to look at me after that veiled compliment. My heart skips a beat, hoping it means what I think it does.

"You gave me something before you left. Can you tell me why?" I ask delicately.

That has his gaze flicking to mine. The fear is back, and I hate myself for causing it, but I have to try. I have faith in him. I know he can do it.

"I…I just…"

"What?"

"I…needed to…" His gaze canvases my face like he's praying I'll provide him with the answer.

"Needed what, Charlie?"

Cheeks ruddy, he lets out a breath like he was holding it. "*You.*"

I can't believe how much I've been waiting and wishing to hear that. Kneading the fabric at his hips, I try to gather my composure. We're not quite finished yet.

"*Needed* me or *wanted* me?"

"I…wanted you with me," he stammers, but then lets out in a rush as his gaze darts around the room, "I don't know why. I just—"

Angling his chin back to face me, I whisper, "I think *I* do."

The way he blinks at me in confusion is so fucking pure and sad at the same time. "Why?" he asks, sounding like he's completely lost.

Oh, Charlie. My sweet Charlie.

Lowering my hands to the tie on his robe, I tug it open. My shiny gift reveals itself when the two sections part.

"Ask me to stay first," I tell his neck, brushing my lips over his pulse. It flutters under my touch. I can practically hear him blushing, so I play unfair and add, "I don't have anywhere to go."

"You…of course you can stay. You're paying for the room."

I have to bite the inside of my cheek, so I don't laugh. Dropping to my knees, I draw the chain out from underneath my shirt and unlock him. Next, I set the combination and gently slide the cage off him. When I lean to the side and set it on the nightstand, I catch his wary expression.

"You don't need this," I assure him, getting to my feet even as he covers himself with his robe.

"But what if…. what if I can't?" He fidgets, shifting from foot to foot. "What if it's not the same?"

"It probably won't be the same. It'll be better."

The doubtful look he makes has me wanting to wrap him in my arms, laugh, and just get to showing him. Instead, I cup his chin and smile, my heart hammering against my ribs. "Do you know why?"

Lower lip slightly protruding, he shakes his head. There's a furrow in his brow above the confusion in his eyes that has my heart breaking for him. Here goes everything.

"Because you love me."

A soft sound of disbelief comes out on a puff of air as his lips part. His breathing immediately goes ragged as his gaze pings all over my face. My God, I am officially the happiest fucking man alive.

"Don't you, Charlie?"

Swallowing, he takes a wobbly step back, looking like he's about to hyperventilate. I could play his knock and answer game longer—wait for him to come to my house each time he can no longer fight his demons—but life is so short. And maybe sometimes people need a little help to figure out what they already know deep down. Reaching out, I grab his hand and follow him.

"And it's *good* that you do," I continue, "so I'm not the only one in love."

He ceases his retreat the second my words are out. He looks like someone just splashed him with a bucket of cold water.

"You…you love me?"

Now, I *do* laugh, taking his face in my hands and giving him a little shake. "God, how could you not know?"

His eyes shift back and forth as though he's looking for some kind of doubt. Typical Charlie. I hear the crinkle of plastic, and the flowers fall to the floor. The next thing I know, his fists are gripping my collar, and he's yanking me to him.

I wouldn't call what he does kissing. It's more like an attack. His tongue delves deep inside my mouth, battling with mine. He whimpers and moves his arms around behind my neck, clinging to me like he's worried I'll disappear. I slip my hands inside his robe and rake them down his back until I have two handfuls of his warm, soft flesh, cupping his ass, and pulling him tight against me.

I kept thinking I had faith he'd come around and would realize what's been building between us, but it's now that I see just how silently fretful I've been over being wrong. I've never had my heart broken, but I think missing out on winning Charlie would have done the trick.

"*Yes*, I love you," I rasp, tearing my mouth away from his to pepper his face. "I think I have since the second I saw you."

Panting, his cheeks bloom again. He lowers his gaze and hands to my chest as though he's not sure what to do next. Placing mine on top of his hands, I guide them to my belt. He sneaks a glance at me, but then licks his lips. He can broker all the deals he wants for me, but seeing that I'm something he's unable to resist is a far better gift.

When I draw my shirt over my head, I feel him start undoing my belt. He flashes me a shy smile. It's the best thing I've ever seen and felt. Running my palms up his chest, I slip the robe from his shoulders as my pants fall to the floor. I kick my shoes and socks off and then turn back the covers.

Charlie hesitates for a moment, like the idea of willingly curling up in bed with someone is foreign to him, but then he musters a smile and slides in under the covers. When I slip in next to him and wrap him in my arms, it makes me sad to see the insecurity return to his face. Except, it doesn't quite look the same as it has before. There's some other emotion there.

"What is it, handsome?"

"Just…why…me? I'm not like you—not…adventurous like you. How can someone like you be attracted to someone like me?"

Stroking a strand of his hair away from his face, I rest my forehead against his. "I don't care about what you have or haven't done, Charlie. People are more than their preferences or zones of comfort. You have nothing to worry about. I'm the one who should be feeling insecure right now. I can't say I regret my behavior, since it got your attention, but I'm pretty sure I've taken the word *obsessed* to a new level," I confess with a laugh, which makes him smile. "The only other cage I've ever even touched was the one I wore years ago."

That has him looking at me in surprise. Settling in closer, I sigh and proceed to shower him with truths his blushes accept as compliments—all the little things that make me know he's the man for me. His work ethic, the way he was so carefree when he joked with Carmen, his mind, and ability with numbers, how he carries himself, and even his discretion and need for privacy. People are often under the assumption that when someone has as much money as I do, they enjoy flaunting their personal lives. I would loathe being with a man who actually wanted to be in the public eye.

And then I tell him about Jeremy and how he reminded me of him. I meant to insinuate that his shyness told me he would be a faithful partner, that he valued love. However, I don't get to. His body goes rigid, and a look of horror crosses his face.

"So, you felt sorry for me? Did you think you were saving me from…from—I don't know. That I'm closeted and miserable and would give up on life because of it?"

Jesus. That did not go where I expected it to, but I understand his assumption.

"No. Not at all," I reassure him, cupping his face. "I'm not collecting Jeremys or trying to replace him or bring him back."

"But…your club. Why would you have a club like that and want a guy like me?"

I blink, soaking in the pain in his expression. God, it makes sense now. No wonder he was wary about wanting to have anything to do with me at first.

"Charlie, I don't hang out at my club. I started it for people to have a safe place to be who they want, to do what they want. Jeremy never felt like he had that. And when I met you, I got the impression that you didn't either. It's why I gave you the card. That's all you have in common. I honestly doubt Jeremy would ever have been able to walk into a place like that. You're brave, Charlie, so fucking brave. I never for a second worried you were the kind of person who would give up on being your true self. I didn't make you go. You went there on your own, again and again." He blushes at that.

"But why didn't you tell me it was you when I talked to you on the yacht? Were you testing me?"

"I wanted to. I had planned to, but when you told me as *me*… as just some guy you were confiding in, that's what really did me in. You trusted me with your secret, which was way more personal for you than trusting some stranger behind a panel with your body. That's when I knew that maybe I'd have a chance with something more than physical with you. I knew we had a physical connection at the club, but you didn't know it was me then."

He gapes at me then, and I'm honestly terrified I've just ruined everything. "You realize that is the most fucked up way to land a guy, don't you? Why didn't you just flirt with me or ask me out?"

Scoffing, I can't help myself, leaning in to steal a kiss. When I pull away, he looks stunned and slightly annoyed. "And that would have worked?" I challenge.

Frowning, he looks too adorable when he pouts. "Probably not," he finally concedes on a grumble, but his fingertip circles my nipple as he says it. "You were a total pain in the ass."

I think that's Charlie-code for admitting my eccentric methods were the best course of action. Smiling, I roll him onto his back and cover him. Kissing his neck, I murmur, "How about I make it up to you by flirting with you every day going forward?"

Maybe I do play a little dirty and test him, because as I say the words, I reach down and stroke his unfettered cock. It's the first time I've touched it in its entirety with my hand, and I know I'm going to enjoy getting acquainted with its smoothness.

"You know me," he mumbles, sounding strained, as I move my mouth down his chest to his stomach. "I don't need any talking."

Chuckling, I plant a kiss just below his belly button. *Nice try, Charlie*. He's not going to get out of being praised that easily. I also happen to know just how much he likes it when I talk. Now, I'm going to do nothing but flirt for the rest of the night.

Moving lower, I rub my cheek against his length, basking in the soft feel of it against my skin. "I love your scent," I whisper. "Especially *here*." Turning, I press a soft kiss to the side of his cock, smiling at how much it's thickened just from the sound of my voice.

"I just…had a shower," he rationalizes, and I try not to chuckle.

"Mm, no, it's more than that. It's *you*. It's your Charlie scent. It drugged me the first time I walked into that room." Rubbing his thighs, I settle between his legs and map a line of kisses down the V of his hip juncture. "If you think about it that way, we could say this is all *your* fault that we ended up here. It was beyond my control. I was…under the influence."

I hear a snort. He fidgets like it's getting difficult for him to hold still. "You're ridiculous."

"I'm glad we understand each other," I purr, just before flicking my tongue over the slit in his cockhead. "And then the way you tasted? Forget it. I didn't stand a chance."

When I capture his tip with my mouth and give its circumference a slow lap, he gasps. "*Fuck*."

It feels so good to be in this bed, soft sheets around me, Charlie's skin against mine. I only dared imagine that it could happen. I knew he could be brave enough to let his inhibitions go for the right man, but as much as I wanted to be, I still worried he wouldn't think I was the right man. My heart swells over the irony that he didn't think he was the right man for me. My mouth is on a mission to prove to him that we fit.

Moving lower, I mouth his sac. It's stiffening already, and I wonder if he knows just how much. His heat greets me when my tongue dances at the base of the seam between his ass. I draw it slowly over that rippled ring, sighing when he lets out a grunt.

Something dusts the top of my head. I assumed he moved the sheets across my hair, but then his fingers brush against my scalp. He grips my hair, hesitantly at first, but then I feel a tug at my roots.

Fucking hell. Yes. He can rip it out for all I care.

Groaning, I move back up and take his entire cock. I am a hundred percent starving to see Charlie go savage. He's solid as steel in my mouth. A drop of his salty essence explodes on my taste buds. God, I want this man—this shy, temperamental-when-he's-scared, sexy-as-fuck man. I love how he looks like the most confident person in any room, and yet gets tongue-tied and rosy-cheeked when he looks at me. I hope he knows I plan on earning that reaction over and over for as long as he'll let me.

"Rory," he gasps, slipping his hands from my hair.

Gripping my shoulders, he tugs for me to come to him. The strength and urgency with which he pulls me up is endearing, considering his earlier doubts about being able to come without his cage on.

Cupping my face, he leans forward, about to kiss me, but then bites his lower lip. I realize I had to pause my flattery because his cock was in my mouth. I can easily remedy that now.

"And every time you bite that lower lip of yours, I want it to be my teeth instead," I whisper.

He lets out a breathless laugh and slowly pulls me to his mouth. I let him do what he wants, giving him time. His lips dust over mine once, softly. And then again. The tip of his tongue taps against my lips, seeking entrance. I open my mouth and let him in. And then he takes. I *love* that he's taking. He moans into a kiss that turns filthy in a heartbeat, and I let my weight settle on him, reuniting my hands with the lines of his body.

When his hips start nudging upward against mine, I wonder how long he'll let it go on. Will he ask? Does he want me to give him those little orders I don't mind giving him? He surprises me, though, breaking free to catch his breath.

"I...I have something. Just a minute."

He slides out from under me and goes to his suitcase in the closet. Turning on my side, I rest my cheek in my palm and admire his bare profile in his crouched position. I get a questioning look when he straightens up with a small bottle of lube in his hand.

"Sorry." I shrug. "I like to smile when I look at you."

Scoffing, he rolls his eyes. I'll make sure he pays for that later. My compliments are to be taken seriously.

Crawling back into bed, he tucks himself back under the covers like a monk preparing for bed. I'm tempted to rip the sheet back so I can see him in all his naked glory, but it's just as sexy to see him trying to act modest while sporting an erection like that.

I didn't miss how he dropped the bottle on the bed between us, as though he did so to free up his hands to situate the blankets, and yet he hasn't moved to pick it back up. Palming it, I find it sealed at the lid. Brand new. Unused.

Oh, Charlie. He really did do soul searching.

"You know," I hum, breaking the seal around the cap, "it's a shame to see this so full. You could have thought of me and used it."

I can barely see his face when he rolls toward me, the way his gaze is fixed on the gap under the blanket between our waists. He looks to be biding his time, patiently waiting to see what I'll do as I dribble some into my palm.

Wetting his lips, he mumbles, "I've tried. It's not the same."

I didn't think I'd be receiving flattery, too, but that morsel of information makes my heart sing. Coating myself with one hand, I tilt his chin up with the other.

"We'll have to remedy that."

His brow furrows. I'd love to know if he thinks that I plan on denying him myself after tonight, or if he's merely doubtful that he can get off on his own just from thinking of me. I can easily clear up both misconceptions.

Slipping my hand between his legs, I lean in and nuzzle his cheek. "It would be good practice for the next time one of us has to take a trip by themselves," I tell him with open-mouthed kisses on the side of his face, working my way toward his ear. "Plus, I would thoroughly enjoy watching you touch yourself while I whisper what I'm thinking."

His breaths come harder as I graze my slick fingers between his cheeks and circle his rim. "Just imagine," I add, nibbling his earlobe. Slipping my index finger into that inferno, he stretches around me easily. "The next time you're away and you touch yourself, I'd be happy to hear all these noises over the phone while I'm missing you. Do you know how hard that would make me, hearing you coming just from thinking about me?"

"Fuck," he rasps, sliding his thigh over my hip and gripping my shoulder. "You're…how do you talk like that…like it's nothing?"

"It's *not* nothing. I mean every word—you bring them out of me whenever you're around." Gripping the back of his neck, I hover over his lips. "I told you…you've become my obsession, Charlie. If there's a cure for it, I don't want one."

This time, he moves in first, claiming my mouth. When he whimpers, I roll us, covering his body with mine. He's solid, all fit muscle, but it's the softness in him now that has me sighing and responding to his hungry kisses.

One of his hands goes to the back of my neck, gripping it tightly. His fingertips stroke anxiously like he's itching to run them through my hair.

Touch me, I want to beg. Touch me all you want, Charlie.

"Do you mind," I preface between kisses, undulating my hips so our cocks slide against one another between us, "that I'm mad about you?"

He makes a strangled little noise. I feel his palm land on my hip. His fingers slink to the soft flesh at my juncture. His mouth breaks away from mine, and he stares at me. His Adam's apple bobs in his throat, and his tongue comes out to wet his lips. The silky flesh of his inner thighs brushes against the outside of my hips, and his hand slips between us, wrapping around me. I think it's the first time he's ever touched my cock unbidden. It makes my throat go thick.

"No," he whispers and angles my cock, so the tip is lined up against his ring. And then…he smiles this shy little smile without looking away.

I practically melt into him with a low growl, pressing forward. I kiss the smile off his face and swallow his gasps. With each inch he accepts, his body cuffs me tighter. When I can't push any deeper, I hug him to me and breathe into his neck.

My skin tingles when his palms slide up my sides and across my back. His soft moan vibrates in his throat against my lips.

"No," he gasps, strained. "I don't mind."

Raising my head, I stare down in gratitude. Cheeks flush from want, his expression is tranquil and full of a look I didn't know could run soul deep. I feel it down to my own, and it brings a tear to my eye. I know it's presumptuous, but at this moment, I know that I'm going to enjoy every second of the rest of my life, and it's all because of him.

I move with purpose. Each draw, each delve, is a calculated art dictated by the sounds and expressions of my lover's body, telling me what he likes best. I don't even have to think about it. I just act on instinct. Making love has never required less thought.

When his breathing and the way his fingertips claw at my back tell me to pick up the pace, I hook one arm under his leg and cup his jaw. "Are you mine, Charlie? Tell me you're really mine."

The desperate words come from a sudden cavern of panic that opens in my chest at the thought of ever losing what I've just been gifted. Is this the fall people say they experience when love comes pounding on their door?

Gripping my hair, he steals my breath with a kiss that goes on until my lungs are burning. "Yeah," he keens. His fingers bite into the meat of my ass, tugging my hips into him. "I'm yours."

His eyes are like an eclipse. I am completely lost in them over those two whispered words.

Mine.

Mine.

Mine.

I don't even realize I'm murmuring it aloud until I catch his repeated, "Yours. Yours," with each slap of my hips.

He raises his other leg, gripping the back of his thigh like he wants more of me. I hook his other foot over my shoulder, nearly bending him in half.

I missed him too much. Wanted the assurance he just gave me too much. The pressure in my cock sends off a flare down my legs all the way to my toes. The next thing I know, I'm helpless to stop the onslaught of my release.

I groan in apology, dropping my forehead to his. Twitching with each pulse, I can barely breathe. Digging his fingers into the back of my shoulder, he makes a sound of beautiful anguish and spasms around me. The added stimulation is almost too much, squeezing me when I'm already on another plane.

His slick cock slides against my stomach with my staggered thrusts; a last-ditch effort to see him to where he needs to be. No metal. No cage. Just Charlie coming between us because of how I make him feel. I am so fucking glad I got on that flight.

I help his legs drop from my shoulders and roll like a felled tree to the side. Panting, I stagger to the bathroom and bring back a towel, blinking through my hazy vision. His stomach is rising and falling with labored breaths. His arms are dead at his sides as he eyes me with droopy lids. I can't believe I'm going to get to see that sight again and again.

Taking the towel from me, he swipes at the mess we made as I slip back under the covers. "I don't think I've ever made an effort to help anyone clean up the way you do," he mumbles off-handedly, tossing the towel to the floor on his side.

Reaching across him, I snake my arm around his waist, pulling him closer. His gaze travels over the sight of me in the bed, and he wets his lips. Probably another first for him, I assume. I refuse to let him go, though. Stretching back, I flick the switch on the bedside lamp, hoping that will help him stay in his happy place.

"Don't worry," I assure him, tugging the blankets up around us. "I'll treat you better than Charlie North."

It was meant to be a playful comment, but his silence stretches in the darkness. He feels tense against me, but then his hand comes up and rests on my forearm. His thumb rakes over the hair there, and he sighs.

"How could I not know what the hell I was doing all these years until you came along?"

The way he murmurs the words and lets out a scoff, I don't think he's expecting an answer. I wait a second to let him absorb his chastisement, pressing a kiss to the top of his shoulder.

"I thought I had it all figured out," he mumbles.

That makes me chuckle. I feel his head turn toward me on the pillow. I can just imagine that severe brow of his, ready to go on the defensive.

"You're not the only one, Charlie. Don't be so hard on yourself. I thought I did, too. I think a lot of people think they have it figured out. There's no room for disappointment when you do. It makes us feel safe."

Slowly, he turns to his side to face me. His fingertips touch my chest and stay there, tracing small circles over my heart.

"I don't want to feel safe," he whispers. "I…I want to be happy."

I squeeze him tighter and cup his cheek. For once, I'm glad the lights are off. If I saw his face right now, it would probably do me in.

"Tell me how and I'll make it happen."

When my thumb traces the corner of his mouth, I feel his lips tick up against my touch. "You already have."

His hand moves, slipping around my waist. As he hugs me close to him and sighs a contented sound, I can feel a smile on my own face.

He rests his head under my chin, burrowing into me. His lips brush against my chest. I barely hear it, but I'll remember it forever. "Thank you for coming. I…I really missed you."

I suck in a breath. My heart thumps hard against my ribs. In Charlie-language, I'm pretty sure that means, *'I love you too.'*

There are no more games. No tests. No fear that can't be overcome. Just a lightness that makes my soul feel like it's floating on air. Pressing my lips to his forehead, I leave a lingering kiss there. A small thank you. Sliding my hand down to his hip, I drag his thigh over mine and settle my leg between his. And that's how I fall asleep, wrapped up in the man who surprised me in a world where I thought nothing could surprise me anymore.

EPILOGUE

Charlie - Seven months later

Shooting off an email on my phone to one of my marketing teams as I walk into the kitchen, I find Rory leaning over the counter, immersed in a crossword puzzle. I will never see the appeal of those brain teasers that have no purpose other than entertainment. They still seem a fitting distraction, however, for a man who loves riddles.

"Don't you look handsome," he purrs, sneaking a glance at me.

I'm in jeans and an old hoodie. He's ridiculous, but I still find my mouth curving up at the corner as I move to the coffeepot.

"Are you ready?"

"Babe, I'm always ready," he drawls, filling in an answer on his puzzle.

Eyeing the line of his back, I follow the slope of his spine down. His long-sleeved Henley is stretched tight across his arms and shoulders. Left untucked at his waist, it's short enough that I get snared on the curve of his ass and how the denim of his jeans is molded to it. No one should look that good in casual attire. I savor the drink he is, and then drag my gaze away. The ideas it gives me are not the kind of ideas I need right now.

Sipping my coffee, I can feel my pulse skitter in my neck. Maybe caffeine isn't a great idea either. Checking the clock on the wall, I can see we still have plenty of time to get to my brother Miles' house, but the visit feels too imminent. Taking my coffee to the sink, I dump the contents of my mug down the drain and let out a calming breath.

Arms slink around my waist from behind, and just the presence of Rory's warm cheek against mine quells the butterflies in my stomach. "Anxious?" he asks, pressing his lips to the underside of my jaw.

"I'm fine." I shrug. "Just…not exactly looking forward to this. You've met my brothers."

"They were charming. Not as charming as you, but I think it went well last time."

His little kisses on my neck are meant to be a distraction, I know. They're almost working. *Almost.*

"Miles and Brett were okay, but they still stared at us the entire time. But Shane? Well, he was a total dick."

"Mm. Good old Shane," he laments playfully, although I don't see how anything about this is amusing. "He was probably jealous."

Rolling my eyes, I turn around to counter his nonsense, but find his arms back around me. That's fine. They can stay. Tracing the seam of his collar with my thumb, I focus on his throat. How can someone's throat be so attractive?

"He's not jealous. He's a homophobic asshole. He has been since high school, and it only got worse when he was in college. He, my dad, and those dickhead friends of his. He'll never be cool with us, Rory. I hope you know that."

I hate the thought of getting disgusted looks at every fami-ly event for the rest of our lives. Rory's parents and his brother Teagan were so accepting when he introduced me to them, I was floored. Our sexuality wasn't even a topic of conversation. I never imagined being welcomed by another man's family was a possibility. It certainly helped with my decision to tell my brothers four months ago. I knew it wasn't going to be as easy, though. Fucking Shane.

"I can't believe you," he had muttered under his breath, when we both found ourselves in Miles' kitchen at one point. Shaking his head as he grabbed another beer from the fridge, he added, "Why are you doing this? Don't you care what people think?"

Why am I seeing a man? Like it was a conscious choice. He's spent too much time with my father, a man whose child-rearing methods were to make his sons hard asses. Thank fuck Miles and Brett saw the light and decided to stay with Mom after the divorce.

"Are you breaking up with me?"

The question catches me so off-guard, my head rears back, and my gaze snaps to Rory's.

"What? No!"

He smiles and hugs me closer, dropping a kiss to the corner of my mouth. "Then I'm not worried about it."

Scoffing, I watch him, stunned. How can he be so nonchalant about all of this? "You don't care that my own flesh and blood is a complete prick and will probably be repeatedly offensive to you for as long as we're together?"

"I'm only worried if he gets in here, Charlie," he says, tapping my temple with his fingertip. "Because if he gets too deep in here and breaks *this*," he adds, running his other hand over my heart, "then he's going to have a problem with me that he'll regret."

The organ his hand is above of wallops inside my chest, and I feel tears in my eyes. Sliding my arms around his shoulders, I bury my face in his neck. "I'm sorry. I just…"

Fucking hate that my own brother can't be happy for me? That he'll eventually take digs at the man I'm in love with?

"I just hate that I can't give you the same type of welcoming into my family that yours did to me."

"If it makes you feel better, Teagan will probably never be fully comfortable understanding my sexuality. He just has manners and loves me."

Manners and love are all I'm asking for, I want to tell him. When he leans his weight against me and steals a kiss, I feel my cage press into my groin, making me hold back a moan.

"Hm…what's this?" he asks, bringing his hand down and cupping over the barrier behind my fly.

"I…just felt like wearing it today," I stammer, pushing away from the counter.

Grabbing my keys off the hook on the wall next to his, I still enjoy the sight of them occupying the same space. I've spent every night here since I returned from France months ago. Two months later, Rory sent a moving van to my house after one of my trips home to change out laundry. I didn't complain. I tried to act like we should think about it, but there was nothing to think about. I didn't want to be anywhere else. When my house sold a month ago, I didn't expect to feel such joy. It made the move feel more permanent. It made *us* feel more permanent.

"Come on," I call to him. "We should get going." Turning back, I find him stalking toward me, hands in his pockets and something dark in his eyes. "What?" I laugh nervously.

"Nothing." He shakes his head with a smirk.

I can tell it's absolutely *not* nothing. It most likely has to do with him catching me wearing my cage for a family function. I only wear it when I have to take a trip, but even then, he calls and says things that…well, I really like wearing it and thinking of those first times months ago.

"I'm just really going to enjoy getting you out of it later," he murmurs, giving my ass a squeeze and guiding me to the door with that hand.

Fucking hell. This shit at Miles' house better not take too long now that he planted that seed. My favorite thing, besides Rory, is when Rory talks me into things.

Two and a half hours later, I'm lounging at a picnic table in Miles' backyard, watching Rory, Miles, Brett, and my nephews play a pickup game of football in the backyard. I am incredibly proud at the moment that my boyfriend is much more athletic than I am. It's just a bonus that he looks really sexy doing it, too, and throwing me a wink and a grin each time he makes a good play.

My ass is starting to ache sitting on this wooden plank, so I get up and stretch. Making my way into the house, I use the restroom and grab another beer from the fridge. So far, today hasn't been horrible. Brett and Miles honestly seem to really like Rory, but I mean, what's not to like? He's a man of all seasons and intelligent beyond words. Even my nephews think he's cool, but his football skills were all that was needed to impress them. Mom flashes me an approving smile as she carts a casserole dish out onto the patio.

"He's a very sweet man, Charlie," she tells me. "You did good."

I find myself blushing at her approval, but I can't disagree. Thank God, though, she doesn't know what that *sweet man* can get up to in the privacy of our own home. Sweet isn't exactly the only word I'd use to describe our home life. He is sweet—sweeter than I ever knew was possible—but my sheltered brain still dubs some of our intimate moments as filthy.

Fuck. Wrong thoughts to have at a family function.

Laughing at myself, I shake my head and reach for a bag of chips on the counter. The front door slams shut, and I hear footsteps. The way my heart sinks, I think I know who it is.

When Shane steps into the kitchen, I suspect this good day has just been ruined. He stops in the doorway as soon as he sees me, his face impassive. Glancing at the patio doors, he murmurs, "Everyone outside?"

"Yeah. The boys are playing football with Miles, Brett, and Rory. Mom just went back out, too."

His expression falls. Glancing back at me, he frowns. What the hell is that for?

"You brought *him* again?"

Him? Is he serious?

"Yeah," I say as casually as I can, trying not to sound pissed off. "He's my boyfriend."

Scoffing, Shane rolls his eyes and stomps out to the backyard. What a dick. Such a fucking dick.

"Shane?" a woman's voice calls. "Where am I going?" A slender brunette appears in the doorway, looking lost and holding a tray of Rice Krispies Treats. "Oh! Sorry." She startles, pressing a hand over her heart. "Hi. I'm Clarissa, Shane's girlfriend."

His girlfriend? What happened to Amy?

"Uh…hi. I'm Charlie. Shane's out back. Here. Let me take that for you."

Showing her through the patio doors, I carry her offering to one of the tables Miles has set up. Clarissa thanks me and scampers off to Shane's side, where he's talking to our mom, who looks equally surprised to be meeting a new woman. It's no secret to me that my brother hasn't ever been faithful to any of his girlfriends, but I thought he was more serious about Amy. I guess I was wrong.

Mom makes her way over to me and whispers under her breath, "What happened to Amy?"

"I…have no idea. As far as I knew, they were still together."

Sighing, she uncovers some of the dishes on the fold-out table and shakes her head. "Not that there was anything wrong with Amy, but this one does seem a little nicer."

Amy had a dramatic flair to her that was tedious at times. She looked high-maintenance if you ask me. I don't know what my brother's type is, but I didn't think he'd go for someone who makes demands on him. I suspected he only tolerated it because she's his boss' daughter. I wonder how his employment is going to work out if he did her dirty.

Someone slaps me on the shoulder. I find Miles panting at my side, his sweatshirt stained with circles of perspiration underneath his armpits. "Your dude is an all-star, bro. Bring him back any time."

The words make pride bloom in my chest even as my face heats over hearing one of my brothers dole out acceptance. I find Rory sauntering over to me, peeling his own shirt over his head. It makes the bottom of his undershirt ride up, revealing a hint of his happy trail. The hair there is sweat-soaked to his abdomen and makes me think of some of the nights our lovemaking was so heated and endless, we both ended up dripping from head to toe.

I lick my lips, unable to help myself.

"Get a grip, Charlie," Shane mutters at my side. "The fucking kids are here. Don't be sick."

Whipping my head around, I resent the way he's not even looking at me as he says it. His gaze is fixed on the array of food on the table. I've accepted over the years that we're a bit of a dysfunctional, somewhat broken family. It's why I tolerate more things than I would at work or in public. I don't ever want to be the one to start trouble, especially with my mom around. She worked too hard taking care of us when I was growing up. But I can't let it go this time. Rory means too much to me. I'm not ashamed of him or of how I feel about him. I put myself through a lot of misery, living with my head under a rock because of people like Shane and his comments. I'm not going to do it anymore. I like being…free. Rory showed me how to do that, and I refuse to tolerate anyone who disrespects the man that gave me that gift. Shane needs to know that.

"I'm looking at the man I love. There's nothing wrong with that. If you're worried about the kids seeing something inappropriate, then maybe you shouldn't have had your hand on Clarissa's ass a moment ago…or is it Amy? Sorry, it's hard to keep track."

It's now that I realize he looks a little worse for wear, as though he hasn't slept well or is possibly hungover. There are dark circles underneath his eyes, and he looks a little thinner than the last time I saw him.

Nostrils flaring, he glares at me. "You know what I meant. You practically drool all over the guy."

Taking a step forward, I get in his space, even though I'm trembling. "I do. Just the sight of him makes my mouth water. Maybe he's right," I venture, giving my rock-solid brother—who could physically kick my ass—a once over, unafraid of his strength for once. "Maybe you're jealous."

He scoffs, and Rory appears at my side just then. Slinking an arm around my waist, he slides in close and gives me a kiss on the cheek. He's panting and smells like sweat—all man. More of a man than my dumb-ass brother standing in front of me right now.

"Everything all right?" he asks, and I smile at his veiled protectiveness.

"Yeah. I was just telling Shane that we'd love to go out to dinner with him sometime."

"Oh, yeah, Shane. That'd be great," Rory enthuses, sounding genuine as always. He slaps Shane on the shoulder, and I take probably too much joy in watching my brother flinch as his face goes red. "We can get drinks afterward, maybe introduce you to some of my friends. There are a few of them that would love you."

"Fuck off," Shane mutters under his breath and turns on his heel.

He barks at Clarissa on his way toward the house that they're leaving. Jesus. What an asshole. Heaving a sigh, I'm not overjoyed by the possibility that I've just killed whatever relationship I have with my older brother, but I feel like a weight has lifted. You can't kill something that wasn't breathing the right kind of life. It's on Shane to repair this, not me.

Arms circle around my waist from behind. Rory nuzzles the side of my face with his. "I take it that means we won't be having dinner with Shane?"

Snorting, I shake my head. Leaning back into him, I let out a sigh. "I'm sorry. He was being a dick, and I lost my temper."

Turning me around to face him, he studies my face curiously. "You don't sound sorry."

"To you I am, not to him," I murmur, tugging at a lock of his hair.

I'm aware my other brothers are still here, as well as my mom and my nephews. I don't think I've ever done PDA in front of them with anyone, but I need it right now.

Brows quirking, he smirks. It's such a good look on him. It highlights that spark of life in him that feeds my soul. "Now, I'm sorry I missed it. Did you just defend my honor?"

"Something like that," I mutter, wrapping my arms around him and burying my face in his shoulder.

"I don't even know what was said, but I bet it was hot," he mumbles against my neck.

Chuckling, I draw back and kiss the playful look right off his face. I can't help but feel proud that he's proud of me for standing up for us.

I hear a wolf whistle. It's followed by Brett yelling, "Get a room!"

I pull back and find Miles and my nephews snickering. My mother has a loving look on her face, and then swats a hand at Brett as she takes a seat by him.

Rory hums near my ear. It's a naughty-sounding hum. "Now there's an idea."

As we join what remains of my family for lunch, I can't help but laugh at his suggestion. I don't know if he's referring to the room

at his club or that hotel room in Bordeaux, but I count my bless-
ings that both had a part in getting me the man at my side.

Later that night, when we're in bed, I take in the sight beneath
me as I slide down on his cock. I will never get over the contrast
of doing this with the image I once had of the kind of man he
was. A stack of books is on his nightstand, along with his reading
glasses, as always. I can't count how many times I've seen his
sleepy eyes nodding off to a book in bed. Peaceful nights where
we've done nothing more than just cuddle and snore. But not
tonight. Tonight, I need him. Need him like this.

I'm fucking exhausted. We stayed at Miles' house way longer
than we had planned to. Who knew that Shane's leaving would
clear the air for more than just me? I've never laughed so hard or
had such a good time. Maybe it was because Rory was there, and
they love him—and I love him.

Maybe it's because I'm different now that I'm with him—the
man I never knew I could be.

On the drive home, we joked about getting a room but decided
that we both prefer the comfort and familiarity of our big platform
bed. It has too many memories in it not to be cherished. One
more of the simplistic things I like about Rory. He has the means
to go and do whatever he wants, but he prefers evenings at home
with me.

Reaching out, he exhales and gives my cock a languid stroke.
I love the look in his eyes when he does that and the way he
seems entranced by the sight of our connection when I ride him.

Smiling up at me, he gives my tip a squeeze that makes me
groan. "You don't look as tired as you said you were."

Snickering, I close my eyes to focus on the pleasure. If he gets
me laughing, I'll never get off.

"I am," I pant, "but I wasn't going to go to bed until you
fucked me."

"Hm. Kind of looks like you're fucking me right now."

Scoffing, I flash him a look, still hating the way he can get me
to blush. "Because you made me."

He didn't. I'm pretty sure I'm the one who rolled us over and
climbed on top of him. The smirk on his face says he knows it.

Stretching his arms above his head and slipping them under
the pillow, he sighs and closes his eyes. "I'm tired too. What can
I say?"

As my thighs burn from bouncing up and down in my crouched
position over him, I wait for him to open his eyes again. He
doesn't, though.

Is he serious?

Scoffing, I tighten my grip on the headboard and lean in. "Playing possum isn't a kink of mine. I can assure you of that."

Stillness. A smirk. Nothing more.

Chuckling, I dig my hand into his hair and press a kiss to his mouth. His lips move, and his tongue slides along mine. When I pull back, though, his eyes are still closed.

"Oh, my God. Knock it off."

"What?" he asks innocently.

"Open your eyes."

"Why? I told you I'm tired. You're doing a great job, handsome. Keep up the good work."

I may hurt him. I give his hair a tug and try not to laugh. "You're hilarious. Open your fucking eyes when your cock is in me."

His lids flare open then. I don't know why, but it gives me a flutter of butterflies in my stomach like the first few times we were together.

"You like when I look at you while my cock is in you?"

I swallow against a thick sensation in my throat. My cock bobs in the air, untouched now with his hand not on it anymore. Taking a slide up, I watch his pupils. When I slide back down, his lids droop slightly, his eyes looking glazed over.

"You know I do," I whisper.

Smiling, he grips my hips and rises into a sitting position. "Hm. I'm suddenly very awake."

Snickering, I shake my head at him and snake my arms around his shoulders. He helps resituate my legs, wrapping them around him.

Planting one hand on the mattress, he cups the other underneath my ass and helps me resume my movements. His head leans in, and he murmurs, "I see you even in my sleep. You know that, right?"

The things this man says, coupled with the way I can take him so deep right now, make my head spin. I leverage my feet against the mattress, riding him with as much gusto as I can for his thrilling words.

"You're a dream that never ends, Charlie. I don't ever want to wake up."

Maybe it was today—the shitshow with my brother Shane. Or the way Rory let me handle my own battle because he always finds a way of making me brave enough to do things on my own. Maybe it's because I haven't said the words enough or that it was a long journey to get me to where I am right now, but I sputter against a sob. I'm so happy and so grateful that I'm literally crying.

"I love you," I blubber, cupping his head and pouring all my emotions into a kiss. "I love you so much, Rory."

The next thing I know, my back is being gently lowered to the mattress. My face is being peppered with slow, soft kisses. Thumbs are wiping my tears. When I blink, I see Rory staring down at me. His eyes are misty, and his face is pure affection.

"And I love you, too," he whispers, dusting his lips over mine.

"Can we go on your yacht next week? Just…get away from everything and go?"

He blinks at me, looking confused. His cock is still inside me, and while we've had conversations during sex before, I realize this is out of the blue.

"I…want a do-over," I tell him, stroking his cheek. "I was a mess when we were on it the first time."

Frowning, he rubs his thumb beneath my lower lip and cups my chin. "We don't get do-overs, babe. That's not how life works. I know it may have seemed messy and complicated—I was a complete savage," he adds, looking guilty. "But I don't want a do-over. I may not have gotten you if it had gone any differently, but," he continues, giving me a soft peck, "I'll take you. I'll take you anywhere you want to go."

As soon as the words are out, I know he's right. My heart feels like it's being squeezed, and my lip starts trembling. I nod and pull him down for a kiss. I wouldn't risk a do-over either. But I will make sure he has the time of his life, and I won't hold back. I'm never going to hold anything back ever again.

I don't let him go, holding him there, deepening our kiss as I rock my hips up into him. He makes a noise against my mouth like he's now sharing this rabid desperation inside me, the kind where we can't get close enough. Drawing my legs up around him, I sink into the pillows as he makes love to me. Slow, steady, hungry, grateful, perfect.

He once told me a piece of ludicrous filth—that my ass and cock were made for him. Granted, I like the thought, but I'm a hundred percent certain now that this man in his entirety—his heart, his mind, body, and soul—was made just for me.

I was living in a cage my entire life before he came along. The key I thought I needed months ago turned out to be Rory's love. It's one I never plan on handing back to him.

DEAR YOU WITH THIS BOOK,

Thank you for reading *Caged By The Stranger*. I hope you enjoyed this first installment of my *Bad Decisions* series. I am always fascinated by how our self doubts and insecurities prevent us from doing or exploring things that may further enrich our lives if we only had the courage. That was my wish for Charlie to overcome with his journey. I wish you confidence on those of your own, whatever they may be.

BOOKS BY DIANNA

The Shutout
The Fating
The Holidate Rescue (novella)
Silent Is The Heart

MEN OF OLYMPUS
You Again
Tough Love

BROKEN HEARTS
Until I Saw You
In The Eye Of The Beholder

CARVER BROTHERS
The Gentleman
The Idiot

GRAND VALLEY
A Fair Warning

Signed copies available at
www.diannaroman.com